SHINE ON, BRIGHT & DANGEROUS OBJECT

Also by Laurie Colwin

NOVELS
Happy All the Time
Family Happiness
Goodbye Without Leaving
A Big Storm Knocked It Over

STORIES
Passion and Affect
The Lone Pilgrim
Another Marvelous Thing

ESSAYS
Home Cooking
More Home Cooking

SHINE ON, BRIGHT & DANGEROUS OBJECT

Laurie Colwin

 HarperPerennial

A Division of HarperCollinsPublishers

Acknowledgments:
Insel verlag: "O Leben Leben wunderliche Zeit" by Ranier Maria Rilke.
Mary Hill Publishers: From "That's How Strong My Love Is."

This book was originally published in 1975 by Viking Press. It is here reprinted by arrangement with Viking Press.

HarperCollins books may be purchased for educational, business, or sales promotional use. For information please write: Special Markets Department, HarperCollins Publishers, Inc., 10 East 53rd Street, New York, NY 10022.

First HarperPerennial edition published 1995.

Library of Congress Cataloging-in-Publication Data

Colwin, Laurie.
　　Shine on, bright & dangerous object / Laurie Colwin. — 1st ed.
　　　　p.　　cm.
　　ISBN 0-06-097632-2
　　1. Title. II. Title : Shine on, bright and dangerous object.
　　PS3553.04783S55　1995
　　813´.54—dc20　　　　　　　　　　　　　　　　　　　　　　　　　94-24622

95　96　97　98　99　　RRD　10　9　8　7　6　5　4　3　2　1

TO RICHARD DAVIES AND LESLIE LONG

O Leben Leben, wunderliche Zeit
von Widerspruch zu Widerspruche reichend
im Gange oft so schlecht so schwer so schleichend
und dann auf einmal, mit unsäglich weit
entspannten Flügeln, einem Engel gleichend:
o unerklärlichste, o Lebenszeit.

—Rainer Maria Rilke

PART I

My husband died sailing off the coast of Maine, leaving me a widow at the age of twenty-seven. This was the time when a lot of girls were losing their husbands to the air war or the ground war; I lost my husband to recklessness, to a freak storm and a flimsy boat. I had no bitter, apologetic telegram to inform me, no grieving soldier at my door with the unsent letter, watch, and kit, no child to console.

His name was Sam Bax, and no one ever stopped him from anything. His brother Patrick and I watched him sail out of Little Crab Harbor when he knew there were storm warnings. We passed the binoculars back and forth, but Patrick got the last full glimpse of him. When he passed the heavy glasses over to me, there was a bright white dot on the horizon, but it might have been a buoy and not the last of Sam's sail. I remember thinking at the time that Sam acted out every wild impulse Patrick had ever entertained and fought down. Sam was thirty, and Patrick thirty-two, the oldest and staidest of youthful lawyers. He executed his violence on the tennis court, and the first time I met him—before Sam and I were married—he and Sam got drunk after dinner and played a vicious game of midnight tennis that ended with Sam's wrist and ankle taped, and Patrick with a dent in his head where he had collided with the racket Sam hurled at him. And that was pretty much the outlet for Patrick Bax. He had squashed his recklessness down to an ironic sort of caution that was a slap in his own face.

Sam, on the other hand, during our five years together,

broke his collarbone when a skittish horse threw him in front of a hurdle, and Sam, who had never jumped, narrowly missed breaking his back and smashing his skull. He broke his right leg skiing, and on a rock climb he cut his shoulder, so deep that, when they carried him down, he was bright gray, unconscious, and you could see bone beneath the wound. I was used to sharing my bed with plaster, tape, and ace bandages. It wasn't athletics, although the Bax boys were athletic in a well-rounded, general way. It wasn't sport at all. If there had been no sports, they would have invented something much more dangerous. They were natural front-line soldiers, but both of them beat the draft by staying where their upbringing dictated they stay—in school—and they graduated as lawyers like their father, grandfather, and great-grandfather before them.

The Baxes summered at Little Crab Harbor, a bleak enclave with a beach composed of lunar-looking rock. From the shore you could see, set on a hump of boulders, the lighthouse at Great Crab, and at night you could hear the bell buoy tolling arhythmically. Their house was a big, rambling, cedar-shingled cottage with a clay tennis court next to the potting shed. All summer long they walked around in smudged whites, their kneecaps powdery gray. All of them—Sam and Patrick and their parents, Leonard and Meridia—were tennis crazy. A little rise, shaded by ash and pine, looked down on the court, and I spent countless hours reading there, or dozing off to the sound of the ball. The Baxes believed in playing until you felt you might collapse. Leonard's face usually turned purple when he had had it, and Meridia became quite yellow under her tan.

But Sam and Patrick never knew when to give up. They kept a big pitcher of water at the side of the net, and they played and drank under the hot sun until the water ran out. Then they held their heads under the pump and returned, dripping, to the court while the air dried them off. If either gave up, it was my turn, but I wasn't much fun for them. I was good for a couple of bracing sets, after which I lost interest and went back to my book. Their usual cry, when I retired to my place under the tree, was "But you were just getting warm!" When I said I wanted to improve my backhand, I could tell they were truly puzzled. That didn't have anything to do with *playing,* they said.

Patrick and I were at the bay window when Sam sailed out. Patrick was annoyed—his chief reaction to his brother. He delivered himself of his standard lecture, referring to Sam as "that collection of accidents." His voice was prim and remote.

"Our Sam is hoping to be elected the world's most dangerous boy," he said. "You shouldn't have let him go. Why the hell didn't you stop him?" He peered through the binoculars. "I wonder if I should put some tarps over the court before it rains."

When he put the glasses down, his eyes were dreamy and angry. You could tell he envisioned himself in that Sailfish, thrilled by the small-craft warning, pitting himself against the sea. It was the end of summer. The leaves were on the verge of turning, and some recent gales had brought down branches. Underfoot, the moss buckled. An hour after Sam sailed out, the sky turned the color of tin and you could see a knot of greenish clouds out by the Great Crab lighthouse. When we went to put the tarps on the court, the air was poised and still, the way it is before it storms.

I said, "I told him not to go. He said it would be his last sail of the season and he wanted me to come with him."

"Sam isn't happy unless someone is worrying," Patrick said. "That's how he keeps his boyish laughter."

As we walked back to the house the wind came up and it began to rain, large, heavy drops that hit on a slant and raised puffs of dust. Patrick spent the afternoon pacing and calling the Coast Guard. I sat leafing through a stack of old salt-bloated magazines, and suddenly I was exhausted: it occurred to me in a rush of panic what I was waiting out.

We had come up to close the house for the year. Leonard

and Meridia were in Boston. I thought we ought to call them.

"I think you should have a drink," Patrick said. "Sam does this every year. He's probably beyond the margin of the storm anyway."

By dinnertime the storm broke, and the winds were fierce enough to knock three bricks down the chimney, splattering the floor with wet soot. At the sound of it I flinched and Patrick's face was as tight as a fist.

For dinner we had ham sandwiches and brandy. Patrick decided that Sam had sailed over to Great Crab and was putting up with Danny Sanderson, one of his tennis mates, but when he called the Sandersons, no one answered. For an hour or so I drank while Patrick drank and paced. The rain let up and then let down in great, incessant sheets. Patrick called the Coast Guard again and I went into the kitchen and wept quietly by the cupboards. When I tried to light the kerosene lamps in case the lights went out, the match trembled in my hand. I was terrified, but if I had presented any part of my fright to Patrick, he would have pushed me away with his restraint. But from the doorway I watched him pace his circle around the braided rug and it seemed to me that his arm's length was justified: he couldn't bear to be ignited. I sat in a chair and watched the storm, and then I fell asleep. It was early morning when I woke up, still dark, and Patrick was asleep on the couch.

The first thing we did was to call the Coast Guard again, but nothing had been sighted. We kept the radio on, and through the crackle of static, we could hear their signals. The water was deep gray and the waves looked hazel. By noon I knew I was going to break down, so I went upstairs and cried in a rocking chair behind the closed door. It was pure fear. When it passed, I looked up and saw Patrick at the door. He looked like someone caught in a wrestling hold.

"Cut it out, Elizabeth."

"I've cut it out. I'm sorry."

"There are only two of us here," he said, presenting me with his handkerchief. "Nothing's happened yet." For the rest of

6

the afternoon, we behaved like people who have broken all their bones but are upright: we avoided any collisions.

Sam's body washed up at Great Crab two days later, and Patrick drove over to identify it. By this time Leonard and Meridia had arrived, but I don't remember Patrick calling them. I don't remember much of the two days Patrick and I spent pinned in that house, startled by the slightest noise, waiting for Sam to call, for the Coast Guard to call, waiting for anything. When the storm spun out, we took turns patrolling the coast. Exhaustion made us level, and we went through two bottles of whiskey and countless pots of coffee. We were as helpless as chickens.

At one point there was an argument between Leonard and Patrick about who would identify the body, but Patrick overrode the responsibilities of wives and mothers and fathers. If he had been challenged, I had the feeling, he would have gone berserk. I asked him if I might go with him and he said, "Just give me this, please," as if he felt this was a horror he should witness and carry through life. I think he wanted me to have a live Sam to think about, but I don't know if it was the Christian gesture it was meant to be. I carried the live Sam with me to share with Patrick, but the dead Sam was Patrick's own.

Attempts were made, by the Baxes and by my parents, to keep me tranquillized with bourbon while what they called "the arrangements" were made, but there was no need to keep me drunk. I was in that state of numbness that suspends energy, and I made pots of tea, pots of coffee, drinks, and sandwiches and passed them around as if I were floating. My parents drove up from Connecticut; Patrick's girl, Sara Lazary, flew from New York; and Sam's grandmother was driven up from Chestnut Hill by a cousin who lived in Philadelphia and left after an hour. The local doctor, George Reeves, appeared with a satchel full of sedatives, all of which were refused by our stoic group, except by my mother, who had the good sense to take a bottle of tranquillizers to keep handy just in case. No one slept, except in fits and starts, and the sleep we got seemed to beat us down. I was crowded by family and they were right to crowd, but I wanted to go off by myself. Since I knew under these circumstances what dramatic weight that gesture would have, I waited until midnight, when only Patrick and his grandmother were up playing solitaire, and then took a long walk on the beach to think about the Bax boys.

They were both filled with blind abandon. In that state, there was no one home in back of their eyes. This proclivity was rampant in both, but in Sam it was almost rompish—as if life were a series of pratfalls from motorcycles. I had always thought it was a fatal condition in Patrick, because he did nothing except play violent tennis with it. There was no joy, no expression—just an intense, concentrated power, like electricity. But it killed off Sam, and at the dining-room table Patrick was playing solitaire with his grandmother, and probably winning. Or he was sleeping dreamlessly, or he was drunk. His grandmother, on seeing me, had said, "I'm used to all this now."

These lean, rough boys stand flanking their parents, Leonard and Meridia, the former Miss Hollander of Chapel Hill and Crab Harbor, Maine, in a photo that used to stand in an enameled frame on Sam's desk. Meridia was lean and flat. She kept her iron-colored hair stylishly short and she had a voice that had been burned by cigarettes into its harsher reaches. She was as stripped and weathered as a plank, but she was chic. From a distance, she looked like an old, jaunty sailor. Up close, she was the New England edition of Coco Chanel. Her lipstick was bright pink against her tan skin, and in the midst of all that weathering her eyes were the stark gray-blue of a child's. She treated her children as if they were gypsies who had dropped in unannounced and had to be dealt with in a civil and efficient fashion, and she probably loved them, but she had always treated them as if they were full grown and did not need the outer symbols of a mother's love. She thought her sons did not want her to fuss over them, and she was right; but, then, she had never fussed.

Her two remedies covered all ailments: a hot shower if you were sick, a cold one if overemotional. Everything at both her houses was immaculate and arranged for comfort, and she was a good, plain cook. When you saw at Little Crab Harbor the wicker baskets of freshly pressed sheets she brought up from Boston, or the bunches of red basil hanging upside down from a beam in the kitchen to dry, or the sheen on her copper pots, or the intelligent books and eclectic pile of magazines she kept in the guest rooms, you thought you were in the presence of domestic splendor. But when you got to know Meridia, you saw she didn't much care. If her boys, or a storm, or a wrecking company with the wrong address had smashed her house, melted down those gleaming copper pots and burned to ash her needlework couch and braided rugs, you had the feeling that nothing would flicker across her face, and as she coped heroically she might make a case for the charm of a spare life. There was not an ounce of sentiment in her, and she doted on nothing she owned. She remembered birthdays, anniversaries, and other ritual events with the aid of a big leather diary in which she noted the upcoming social events of her life. Meridia had replaced feeling with efficiency: it served her very well and it looked like the same thing. Sam's drowning was only a hard, harsh fact in her life.

Her indomitable competence was calculated to make things work so smoothly that she didn't have to think about them, and when you looked into those large blue plates she had for eyes, you wondered what her connection to the world was. She lived in a universe in which things were brisk, cheery, and workable. You could not imagine her giving in to pain or weeping with joy, and nothing distressed her. The people she knew did not divorce, or die young, or get kidnaped, or commit crimes. She used her remoteness like a shield, and Sam, her youngest, understood his mother about as well as an unborn child understands quantum mechanics. Patrick said of her, "Some women want only sons, but a daughter or two might have softened her up."

Leonard was tall and silent. His legs were thin and his knobby knees were the size of ashtrays. He was all edges, but

9

they were comfortable edges. However, he was not the sort of man you want to hug. His eyes were a dark, unyielding brown. Sam and Patrick understood their father: after all, they were just like him. They were lawyers, tennis players, landowners in Maine. The prep school they had gone to he had gone to, and they had graduated from his college and his law school. From Meridia they got their thick, wavy hair and the roundness of their eyes, but everything else was Leonard's. They had his flat nose and cheekbones, his build and leanness. But their fleetness and danger were all their own.

I was twenty-one when I met Sam. He came roaring down from Cambridge on a Vincent Black Shadow with Eddie Liebereu, the boy it was assumed I would marry. Eddie had been the shining star of my high school. He was a Merit Scholar, a Westinghouse fellow, the editor of the newspaper. He was three years older than I, and it was quite the thing to have a crush on him. We spent a summer together teaching retarded children how to swim, and the rest followed a safe, comfortable pattern. When he went to college he wrote me letters which I answered within four days. Each letter took at least five drafts before I thought it suitable to send to Cambridge. At holidays he appeared and took me to parties, receptions, concerts, and lunches. He sat at my parents' dinner table and I sat at his. Under the table, concealed by lace and damask, we played benign footsie. Over the anemones his mother favored and the freesia my family used for a center-piece he winked at me. In my senior year of high school, he got me up to Harvard for a weekend after this was cleared by my mother through Mrs. Liebereu. He took me by the elbow and squired me through Harvard Yard, through Harvard Square, past shimmering pairs of older girls I incorrectly assumed he was sleeping with. He steered me through the Fogg Museum and gently explained to me the significance of Gentile da Fabriano. How could I have seen him for so much Harvard Yard? In my second year of college, Eddie took me to his apartment and thus became my first lover, and it was assumed that he would be my first husband, but by that time my life was fairly divided. We had to commute to get to each other,

10

and in our times apart, a hidden but audible voice indicated to me that tame Eddie Liebereu was not the love of my life at all.

When Sam appeared with him, I knew at twenty-one that I was a gone woman for sure. How we conspired to dump Eddie at the library and leave him there for the afternoon, how we managed to convince him that a motorcycle ride with Sam would be an educational experience for me, how we managed to get him to leave the next day, and how I managed to treat him so awfully and live with myself I cannot imagine. We did all these things. With my arm around Sam's waist, racing down the River Road, I felt that I was a flame and Sam was a flame, and that I did not belong in a world of candle snuffers and wet pockets like Eddie Liebereu.

It was late October, and the leaves along the Hudson River were bright yellow. We sped by large abandoned barns, past trees that looked like burning bushes, and finally we pulled into a seedy bar and grill by the ferry docks in Michaelstown for a beer.

"What's with you and Eddie?" Sam said. "Are you trying to get rid of him?"

"I wasn't trying to get rid of him until this morning. I'm supposed to love him, but I can't."

Sam said, "Wanna come up to Cambridge and stay with me next weekend?"

"Yes," I said. I was pretty daring at twenty-one.

"Wanna put him on the train and spend the rest of the weekend with me?"

I said I thought that was just what I wanted. We left the bar and roared off back to school until we came to a dirt road that led to an apple orchard. Sam leaned his bike against a tree.

"Don't you think we ought to seal this bargain with a kiss?" he said, and then, "Are you sure you want to do this?"

"Are you?"

"I'm sure if you're sure."

"I'm perfectly sure," is what I said.

Sam had soft, thick, floppy hair. Washed, it felt like wilted lettuce, and as it dried it waved. At times he was so thin you could see the bones in his back, but he was too sturdy to be frail or anemic. He was filled with random, haywire energy. The next weekend I went to Cambridge, and until I graduated I commuted, happy, hyper, giving alarm to those at home. But I had found my proper heat and center: Sam and I formed our own elite.

Even in those early days, my large range of feeling for Sam included an unimplemented protectiveness. What it came down to was that I was frightened for him, and in soppier moments I used to say little prayers for his safety. I put up with the lousy train from my college to Boston so as to spare Sam the chance to wreck his motorcycle on the Thruway and I bought him a gold St. Christopher's medal, which he laughed at, but wore.

Even at the start, I thought how young and daffy we were. How could we have known what we were doing? In love, we were like a pair of orphans in a story by the brothers Grimm, charming waifs against the cruel outdoors. Our wedding could have been the marriage of two colts. The word for us was adorable. It amazed me that at the age of twenty I had conducted a love affair and at twenty-one decided who the love of my life was and at twenty-two made a marriage. When I think of our apartment in Cambridge, I think of a set of rooms in a playhouse, with all our trappings and wedding presents gleaming on the shelves. We did what adults do—we had the newspaper delivered, we entertained, we washed the windows, took showers, dressed ourselves. Sam finished his last year of law school and I did graduate work in music. We had friends in for dinner. But sometimes it was hard for me not to picture me and Sam as two damp children bending over a toy car, absorbed and brainless, in the middle of a leafy road.

II Sam's funeral was tame, and eccentric. We closed up the Maine house and drove to Boston in a cortège. I drove with my parents and Sam's grandmother. Meridia drove with Sara Lazary and Patrick drove with his father. My father and Leonard had arranged to have Sam's body flown down to Boston airport and picked up by the tasteful firm of Merwick and Levada, Morticians. I was not sheltered from these details, but I had to ask for them, and was told what I wanted to know by Meridia or my mother, in the way the facts of life are gently and soberly explained to children. These encounters made me realize that Sam was now a black star, or a piece of side meat that had to be quickly dealt with before the sun spoiled it further.

Sam was to be cremated, as he had once told me was his wish, although his ashes were not going to be scattered over the Yucatán peninsula, as was also his wish. He was going to the family plot in Moss Hill, Massachusetts. Sam would have liked a monster booze-up and a little keening, since his sentimental preferences ran to the loud and garish. He had once been to a wake—one of the great parties of his life, he said.

The service was held at the cemetery and we spread out over the grounds, dotting the dark-green grass in our black clothes. Sam's ashes were placed in a vault in the mausoleum of his grandfather Cyrus Bax. The minister read from Keats, and my father recited the Kaddish, a prayer Sam claimed to love in deference to my origins. Two days before the funeral I had gone by myself to a stonecutter in Roxbury who had chiseled on a thin, white marble slab:

> Samuel Pattison Bax
> And Death Shall Have No Dominion
> Rest in Peace

and his dates.

It had rained very briefly in the morning, and the sky was the weatherbeaten color of old barns. It was the sort of day on which you can read the inscriptions on the insides of antique wedding rings. We passed rows of Hewitts, Hulls, Tapleys, and Goldsmiths; passed graves so old that the headstones were wafer thin but you could see the eroded outlines of those gawking angels the Colonists were fond of.

Cyrus Bax's mausoleum was black marble. Perched on the top of it, like a resting sparrow, was a mournful little cherub. We stood under the trees with our heads bowed. When I lifted my head I saw that everyone was unhinged by grief. Even Sam's grandmother, who was used to all this—having buried a husband, a sister, and most of her friends—seemed to cave in. She understood the passing of the aged, but not the wipe-out of the young. Patrick was standing closest to me, and I could see every line in his face. He stood so stiffly I was afraid a breeze might knock him over. The rays around his eyes—all the Baxes had them—looked deeper. After the minister finished and the Kaddish had been said and Danny Sanderson had placed the white marble slab over the vault, no one knew what to do next. If it had not been a funeral, if we had not all been cloaked in black, we might have been guests waiting for the picnic baskets to be opened—it was that bucolic.

But someone was supposed to speak. I didn't remember until he came forward that it was Henry Jacobs, Sam's professor of constitutional law. He was a small man in a sober banker's suit and he was the only adult I had ever heard Sam express constant liking for. His classes were the most popular at the law school: he was quiet, but passionate, and underneath his great seriousness, he was impish. The several times

14

he had come to our apartment for dinner, it was like entertaining a Talmudic scholar from another century.

When he stepped in front of that huge mausoleum, he looked like a garden gnome. I wondered if Meridia and Leonard found it strange that their son had married a Jewess and was being eulogized by a scholar wearing a skull cap.

Henry Jacobs blinked at the glare and began.

"We come in sorrow today to bury our dear Sam, our lovely boy. He was son, brother, husband, student, and lawyer. May God in his infinite mercy and justice look upon his soul with all the love deserved it."

His voice was shaking. There were large spaces between all of us. No one wanted to be near. I could feel the wet grass through my shoes. When Henry Jacobs called Sam "our lovely boy" I bent my head and tears streaked down my cheeks, one after another.

"Dear Sam, your presence taught us fleetness, the joy of being mobile. Let us not ponder what could have been, but try to rejoice in what was. May we all learn from your life the sweetness and glory of a passionate spirit and may we think of you when our courage falters. May God bless you and keep you."

When he turned to me, his face was wet and slumped and so was mine. I was amazed at him: he was the eccentricity at the service. Even Meridia, who was generally impassive in public, looked astonished and moved. I was terrified that I would burst into tears on Henry's shoulder. My crying had been done in private, in the shower with the water running down so I could howl unabashedly. I was afraid that if anyone let go in the midst of this poised silence, no one would be able to carry on, or get through the days to follow.

Danny Sanderson had given me a bunch of lilies, and as people started to leave the graveside, I put my lilies in front of Sam's plaque. I didn't want him to rest in peace. I wanted him to bounce around in death as he had in life, fearless, goofy, and fleet.

The Bax house was packed when we got there. My mother,

who knew her way around Boston, had ordered catered sandwiches and cakes, and my father had attended to Leonard's liquor supply. It was a sign of how far gone the Baxes were that my parents had been allowed these gestures: Leonard and Meridia never let anyone do anything. I was elbowed by aunts and cousins, patted on the arm by the people from Sam's firm, taken aside by friends with offers of country houses if I needed shelter, and I was talked up quite a lot. No one wanted to talk about Sam at all: the idea was to distract the attention of the bereaved, but I didn't want my attention distracted, and as the afternoon went on, I felt awkward and distorted. I had had Sam for five years, but Meridia and Leonard had lost a son, and Patrick a brother. I was only a relatively recent wife.

My parents and the Baxes sat on the sofa, and respects were paid to them. Danny Sanderson cried with his arms around me and then went home, drunk and tranquillized. When I tried to tell Henry Jacobs how grateful I was to him, he waved me away and said, "Come see me in a few weeks and we'll talk." When I left the living room he was talking to Meridia and my mother. Then I went to find Patrick, who had disappeared.

I found him in the attic, which had been the playroom when he and Sam were boys, shooting darts from nine feet.

"I'm sorry I deserted you," he said. "I realize we're the guests of honor, but I really can't take all that shit."

I sat on the edge of an armchair and watched him shoot. He and Sam were fanatic dart players when the weather kept them indoors. He was shooting 'round the clock, but hadn't got past six.

"I don't mean to defame the occasion," he said. "But I'm sure Sam would have wanted me to play darts."

I said, "Stop it, Patrick."

"Actually, it's a very good outlet. Isn't that what they're calling it these days? You ought to try it, although I don't remember your being very good, or were you?" He had given up 'round the clock and was shooting for bull's eyes.

"Here," he said, handing me the darts. "You get to shoot from seven feet since you're smaller."

16

We shot for half an hour, but neither of us was much good. Patrick was slightly drunk, and although we avoided looking at each other, I know the board was swimming for both of us. Our shots got more and more awry and we were both crying without making any noise. Patrick seemed crippled with grief. I asked him if he wanted me to get Sara, but he told me she had gone back to New York.

When the afternoon crowd left, the evening crowd arrived. In the kitchen, Meridia, my mother, and I discussed why they felt I should not go back to my apartment—mine and Sam's. I had spent three nights at the Baxes' and had been home only to change my clothes. I said I wanted some time alone and they were forced to understand, since they did too.

At the end of that long day, there was a lot of clutching. Meridia had me by the arm and my mother had me by the hand. They were both exhausted and I felt like a hammock holding up two pillars. Leonard and my father sat silently on the couch, sipping whiskey and smoking their pipes.

They wanted me to stay because they wanted me around: I was their direct link to Sam; I was his memento. And they were probably afraid that I might shoot myself, left alone with all Sam's things. Patrick drove me home, while I added guilt to grief.

I said, "Was it wrong not to stay?"

"It's hardly polite for the bereaved to walk out."

"For God's sake, Patrick."

"It's okay. Anything is okay at times like these."

"I just couldn't take it any more."

"I'm sure they understand perfectly."

"I just want a little space for myself," I said.

Patrick's knuckles were white on the wheel. "Elizabeth. Shut up."

We were both severely whipped. It is awful to know that your catastrophe involves everyone else. It allows you no safe haven: there is no one available for sheer comfort, since the people you most want are mourning too. I shut up and we drove in silence, but when we got to the apartment, Patrick followed me in. He didn't want coffee or a drink. We sat

17

around, too manic to sleep, too tired to say anything. I told him if he wanted to stay, I would make up the sofa for him. He only nodded so I brought out the bedding and put it on the couch.

"Do you want to go for a drive?" he said.

"I want to drink some bourbon and go to sleep."

I made him a cup of tea, and when I brought it to him, he was pacing. He looked more like Sam than I had ever seen him—like Sam at his most restless. His hair was flopping onto his forehead, his eyes were slightly wild, and his shoulders were so hunched with tension the blades almost touched. He took a few sips of tea, paced some more, and then he stopped, and hurled the cup at the wall. It shattered, leaving a large, watery stain.

I put my arms around him, and he held me so tight I thought I would stop breathing. He didn't make a sound, but his entire body shook. We were so close you could not have passed a thread between us, and when we pulled apart, the collars of our shirts were wet with tears.

I said, "Go to bed, now, Patrick."

He bedded down in Sam's pajamas, and when he was under the covers I sat beside him and stroked his hair until he closed his eyes and seemed to be asleep, but when I got up, he took my hand and wouldn't let go. I didn't want to go. He was Sam's brother. Up close, he smelled like Sam, of grass and soap. I lay down beside him and he curled his arm around my waist as you would clutch a newspaper in a windstorm to keep it from blowing away from you. We slept like spoons, and I kept waking. He was restless in his sleep, fevered and damp, but he kept his arm around me. It was like sleeping next to drying clay.

Hours before, I had put my lilies on Sam's grave. I didn't want to remember, but I did. Memory is sensual, not logical. I could see the lilies, their velvety insides and the smudge of pollen they left on the front of my black dress. I remembered the set of Henry Jacobs' shoulder as he walked to the cars with Patrick. I remembered that we looked like a group of people who have been rained on, not like the victims of real grief. It was a terrible, unspeakable loss. It made me want to crack my head against the wall and yowl, but I was pinned to Patrick. I didn't want to wake him, but I couldn't keep from crying. I held myself so stiffly the tears forced their way out of me and although Patrick didn't wake, he turned around in his sleep, put his arms around my neck, and sighed.

When I woke up, our arms were still entwined. He was sleeping and I felt slightly cooked, he was so warm. It was raining. Dim light flickered in. The tea stain had dried on the wall. Patrick stirred, and I stirred. I wanted to get up, but he held me down. Then he kissed me on the mouth, pushed me away, and fell asleep again.

I took a shower, dressed, and while I was making the coffee, I heard him get up, and heard the water running in the bathroom. Then he appeared, red-eyed and dressed, his hair slicked down the way Sam slicked his hair down when it was wet.

"You know," he said, "it's a blessing in disguise, this business. It spared you the misery of eventual divorce."

I hit him open-handed in the face. He went pale, but he was not surprised.

"But you have to admit, it's true," he said.

And I had to admit, the day after Sam's funeral, it probably was.

III No one was remarkably happy when Sam and I decided to get married. No one took us very seriously. Patrick treated us with the scorn you might deal out to children overstimulated at the movies. My mother wondered if the Baxes would mind having Jews in the family, but they didn't care one way or the other. Meridia seemed to be slightly worried for me. Leonard and my father, who referred to Sam as "that kid with the motorcycle," thought weddings were for women, children, and dogs, so they paid the bills and smoked their pipes.

In the end, they married us off as if we were some curious but not very interesting experiment in hybrid roses, and there was obvious relief all around. Sam, as we knew, was the unspoken trial of his family. Hadn't he broken almost every one of his bones? Didn't he own a motorcycle so huge and fast it couldn't be insured? Hadn't he been known to get drunk and sprint over hedges or drive his car in reverse at fifty miles an hour down one-way streets? But Sam knew where his real obligations were. He had gone to school like a good boy. He had gone to college and graduated magna cum laude. He had made the law review and was attached to a good firm. Those were the things that counted, so there wasn't much Leonard and Meridia could hang him for, and thus they knew they had no reason for concern.

But was I concerned? Sam wasn't mine. He was his own. I often felt that I had won Sam the way you win the lottery: there were no conditions to your luck. Only after the fact did I realize how scared I had been, and how out of a bundle of fear I had knitted an impossible sort of tolerance.

The easiest thing to produce in others is guilt, and Meridia was an artist at it. She did it subtly: her eyes looked pained, but she knew the effects of good soldierism, so she never said a word. Things wounded her only in her silent heart, whose chambers beat with the blood of approval or disapproval, but she would never state her case. The lines on her forehead showed you that she accepted things with dead-set finality, and she suffered for it. With this she trussed her youngest up like a chicken, and smiled benignly upon him so that he might feel, but never know, whatever it was that bothered her. That benign smile kept him guessing.

The love of Sam's life, before he met me, was a girl called Jocelyn Heathers, and from what he told me I figured she was the queen of the guilt producers. Between Meridia and Jocelyn, Sam sweated and stewed in his own sense of wrong. Jocelyn admired the freeze-out, the silent treatment, the slow burn. If Sam was rowdy at a party, didn't call when he was meant to, wanted to go camping with his pals, got drunk, passed out, talked dirty, or belched at the symphony, Jocelyn withdrew heavily. Her code of conduct was elaborate and rigid and Sam broke her rules one by one by one. Like Meridia, she never articulated her disappointment, but her reaction was precise while Meridia's reactions were imperceptible but far more effective. They wanted him to be a different boy, he thought. I, on the other hand, wished he were less reckless, less willful, but I never said so because Sam was Sam, and that was my part of the bargain. If he had made himself less reckless, less willful, wouldn't he have *been* a different boy?

Jocelyn Heathers, whom Patrick called "that jolly hockey-stick," was the sort of girl Sam hung around with before he met me. She looked like someone in deep thrall to field sports, was large, blond, and woodsy. Her hair was as straight as a guitar string and altogether she was as ruddy as a brick fireplace. Together they went hiking, skiing, and backpacking until Jocelyn realized that Sam's notions of good clean fun were not hers. It was not her intention to find the most dangerous crags during a rock climb and perch on them with the tip of one unsteady foot. She did not wish to swim out beyond the breakers. Jocelyn studied political science and was a solid Democrat. After she and Sam broke up, she married a medical student called Denton McKay and moved to Maine. When Sam died, she sent me a note of condolence written on her husband's prescription pad.

I used to hear quite a lot about Jocelyn Heathers in the early days of me and Sam. Patrick said that Sam was glad to put in an earnest day of hell raising, because at the end of it would be Jocelyn, who would either pout, freeze, or otherwise manifest her pained displeasure. It seemed to me that she had preyed on every one of Sam's bad impulses. She took him by the scruff of his lovely neck and barbecued him. Everything I had constructed an intricate morality to avoid doing she did. He spent his time with her in a state of contrition, and Sam contrite was hateful. I didn't care if he tooled off with his pals or gave himself a massive drunk when he passed the bar exam. I didn't care because we were co-conspirators, and Sam checked in every several hours to assure me he was still alive. After one night of spectacular boozing in one of his scuzzy bars, he took a long shower and appeared with his hair slicked down, looking like a guilty choir boy. He presented me, slightly pigeon-toed and wearing an expression of doglike mournfulness, with a large bunch of anemones. Then he took me out to dinner and spent the first course staring at his plate.

"What's wrong with you, Sam?"

"I'm sorry. I'm just really sorry."

"What for?"

"For getting drunk."

When he lifted his eyes from his congealing steak, I saw that he really was sorry, and I was about to say it didn't matter, which was true. But he wanted to be sorry. He wanted me to be angry, and it would have been cruel of me to take the edge off his apology, so I accepted it, which seemed to cheer him.

Jocelyn hated that everything he did excluded her, even if they were together. She was frightened on the back of motorcycles. Her athleticism had to do with cheerful competition. Sam's good times were not her idea of a good time and, for all that, she wasn't a very gentle girl. She wanted Sam to haul off and slap her, and she perceived his recklessness as a form of brutality that she was all too eager to exploit, or else what was she doing with him? But I was a fan of recklessness. Gentle and contained Elizabeth liked the thrill of whipping down the River Road behind Sam. I liked driving too fast myself, and I loved a hairpin turn when I could find one. But, day to day, I just loved Sam. I loved him for himself, so how could I restrict what he held dear? His energy was a beautiful thing to me: it was bravery. Hadn't I been brave? Hadn't I chucked a tight, safe life with Eddie Liebereu? Didn't I believe that safety lay on the side of those who made a pact with danger?

The little Marcus girl, Elizabeth Olive, nicknamed Olly, married the nice Bax boy and went to live in Cambridge with her husband, pursued her studies in music and composition, and continued her faithful practice of the piano. They unpacked the Spode, the silver, the sheets and towels. They unpacked their separate college possessions and hung their clothing side by side. The bride learned to fish, bought hiking boots, and listened to the Top Forty during the many drives she and her husband took. The groom learned to sit still for more than five minutes at a time, was introduced to the basics of cooking, and began to hum parts of the Mozart sonatas his wife played for him on the piano. The friends of the happy couple came trooping in and out and took the happy couple for granted. They were in great demand at parties since they could be counted on to dance. The groom's brother came for dinner and watched over his sister-in-law as if she were a species of rare moth, and, all in all, they racked up quite a lot of photographs. Dark, skinny Olly smoking a cigarette on a boulder; Olly, Sam, and Patrick in front of an enormous Victorian mirror; Sam and Olly in bathing suits; Sam and

Patrick carrying fishing rods and wearing straw hats; Olly surfcasting; Sam, Olly, Patrick, and Sara Lazary in tennis whites smiling like polite children; Sam by a window; Olly by a window; Olly and Sam as bride and groom; Henry Jacobs and Sam bending over a stack of papers. Olly asleep. Sam asleep. Sam throwing a stick to an unidentified dog at Little Crab. Olly with someone's cat on her lap. The Marcuses. The Baxes. The in-laws together, linking arms. Sam with a wreath of flowers on his head, looking faunlike and devilish. Sam in a top hat. Sam walking down the beach alone. Sam and Patrick standing on the Sailfish Sam was killed in.

Half the world that cared thought it a tragedy that the Bax boy had died so young. The other half thought it was a miracle he had lived to see thirty. Both halves checked in, by letter and by telephone, but mostly by letter. The postman was so overburdened that for two weeks he walked the two flights and delivered the mail by hand.

"I sure was sorry to hear the bad news, Mrs. Bax. You get to know the people on your route and I used to see that husband of yours going off on that motorcycle of his." He handed me a bundle of letters. "I guess there's nothing I can do, but I sure feel bad. I can see you got a lot of friends, so I'm glad to bring you all these letters."

His name was Mr. Almonides, and I thanked him.

But the cards and letters, the bunches of flowers that appeared daily, filling vases, water glasses, and eventually milk bottles, the silence of the apartment, the rack of useless clothing in the closet—none of this informed me. It was too much at once. I wanted to pack up and leave, to go on to the next step, not to escape but because I knew I was going to pay heavily and I wanted to do it on my feet, in action. No week of breakdown, of intense weeping would have cleared my head. My mourning was going to be done over the long haul.

After I hit Patrick in the kitchen, we sat down and had a civilized breakfast in which neither of us had much interest. We went through two pots of coffee and read the papers. Patrick didn't make any move to leave, and I didn't want him to go. At midday, it began to rain heavily. By two o'clock we were jangly and over-coffeed.

"Let's take a drive," Patrick said, and we walked through the rain to his car. We drove into the country without saying a word, listening to the swish of the windshield wipers. Patrick turned off down a muddy lane and stopped the car. The rain brought down leaves, pasting them against the windows.

"In a few days, you're going to be subject to a pow-wow," Patrick said.

"What does that mean?"

"It means that Leonard and Meridia will want to know what you want to do."

"That sounds like they want to give me a hundred bucks and tell me to leave town," I said.

"Don't be so melodramatic," said Patrick. "Your parents want to know too, and so do I."

"How do you know I want to do anything?"

"Because you'll want to do something."

I said, "I could stay in Cambridge and study music."

"Is that what you want?"

"Sam had a job offer in New York. We were thinking of leaving Cambridge anyway."

"Do you want to live in New York?"

"I don't know."

"I'm there," said Patrick. "You have friends there."

"I want everything to be normal," I said.

"Well, it isn't."

"Would you like it if I came to New York?" I thought he would say it was up to me.

"Yes, I would," he said. "It would probably be good for you to get out of here, but I asked more for my sake than for yours."

When I asked what he meant, he started the car and began to drive home. Patrick, when silent, was shelled up like an oyster.

"It would be nice to have you around," he said, and it was clearly all he had to say.

Part of Patrick was methodically businesslike, and part of

me was practical. We dealt with Sam's clothing a week later, and Leonard called to ask about what he called "the effects," a word I found quaint, but which he used almost obsessively. The more he talked, the more I had the feeling that nothing of Sam's was mine—it was only Sam's and now that there was no more Sam it was rightfully the Baxes. After all, Leonard had always been Sam's father, but I had only intruded into Sam's life. Leonard didn't mean to make me feel this, but I felt it. I told him that I didn't know what to do with Sam's things, that I did not consider them mine, that there were a few things I wanted and the rest, if they liked, was theirs.

"You are Sam's widow," said Leonard, who was a lawyer to his marrow. I said I would talk it over with Patrick.

Patrick was the only person I could bear to see, and he didn't want any of Sam's clothes—he was slightly taller and not so manically skinny—so we boxed and bundled them and gave them to the Salvation Army. Danny Sanderson asked for his leather jacket, and when I gave it to him, we both wept. Danny was Sam's perfect friend: dumb and loyal, fall guy and straight man. He was as rough and risky as Sam, but if you saw them race off together, Sam on his Black Shadow and Danny on his sleek Ariel, you thought that one was sitting in the side car of the other. When his master died, poor Danny was struck deep in his unintelligent heart. He knew at least one thing about love and friendship, and he suffered.

I kept two sweaters, a rugby shirt, a braided belt, and a suede jacket Sam had gotten for his sixteenth birthday. I started packing up the rest on a Saturday, and packing up those clothes knocked me backwards. Patrick came over and sat himself in front of the television to watch a football game. He didn't want to help: he wanted to be around, and I was profoundly grateful to him. I didn't want help. I wanted his presence. There was only one way to face Sam's mismatched socks, suits, shirts, handkerchiefs, and shorts, and that was to face them. There is a point at which true grief and sentimentality meet. I tried not to, but I wept all over his clothes.

It probably would have been a comfort if I had been able to

convince myself and anyone in listening distance that Sam had abandoned me for death, that he had left me stranded in the springtime of our tender lives. There were times when it would have been easy to collapse on the shoulder of Danny Sanderson, or any of Sam's goofy, stricken pals and mutter such heartfelt and sympathy-producing sugar roses. What grief teaches is that its most convenient and endurable form is pure greeting-card sentimentality. I didn't want sympathy, or pats on the head, or the arms of comparative strangers encircling me in the face of an event so serious it did not need embellishment. As the days went by, I realized that grief is metabolic: it crawls through you like disease and takes your energy away. Then it gathers and hits like sudden migraine, like being hit by a car, like having a large, flat rock hurled at your chest.

It would have been easy to tote up my loss among all those shirts and socks. I could have done some mournful brooding over Sam's tan suit—the last time he had worn it, and how we had gone out for dinner and a walk in Boston Common. I could have tried to remember what he said when he put on the green silk tie Meridia and Leonard brought him back from Paris, or the bright red-and-pink socks my parents found for him on a trip to Peru. But it seemed a pain so easily summoned that I didn't trust it. There is a part of mourning that wants to be done unencumbered and in peace, that wants to be done in a spare white room, with nothing familiar around.

I found in his pockets the keys to his motorcycle, four dollars and sixty-five cents in loose change, a ticket stub to a Boston Celtics game, a cleaning bill, a postcard informing him that his lighter had been repaired. In the living room, Patrick had dozed off. It was halftime at the football game, and on the gray-and-white field a group of girls were tossing batons into the air while the crowd cheered. Patrick sat formally on the sofa, but his limbs were slightly askew, as if he had been thrown there like a rag doll. There was no expression on his face except the traces of exhaustion, and the sight of those inky lashes against his pallor made me feel a shot of tenderness, he looked so frail. He was wearing gray trousers and a white shirt with a frayed collar, and he looked uncomfortable. When he woke up, it was as if he had slid out of sleep.

"There are some things I think we should go over together," I said.

"Like what?"

"Family things. Your grandfather's watch chain, some cufflinks, stuff like that."

"I don't want them," said Patrick. "You keep them."

"They don't belong to me."

"What you'll find, Elizabeth, is that everything belongs to you."

"It's wrong for me to have them. They belong to your family."

"Then give them to Leonard, for Chrissake." He realized he had shouted, and apologized. "Look, my parents are a pair of sticks, but you have to remember that you were Sam's family, too."

Then he said, "Does Sam have any handkerchiefs? I seem to remember he had some fancy ones from England. I'll take those."

He went back to the football game and I went back to the closet. There was a small trunk of clothing Sam had gotten bored with, and three years before we had spent an afternoon trying to decide what should be thrown out. Sam didn't like to throw anything away: that meant you had to make a decision about it. But since they were his clothes and something had to be done about them, he got quite into the spirit of the thing. If I found something that was worn, patched, and two sizes too small, something he hadn't put on his back for seven years, his interest peaked immediately. He was filled with the notion of sentimental value, and he spent the afternoon saying, "No, keep it. We'll put it in the trunk. I always liked that tee-shirt. I'll get around to it. You never know when you'll need an extra windbreaker and if I take those loafers to the shoemaker, all they need are new heels and soles and some stitching and they're perfectly reasonable. Besides, I wore those loafers to a dance once."

28

I hadn't touched that trunk since. When I went through it, I found in the pocket of a torn workshirt a note I had written to him before we were married. It was dated, and it said:

> S: I kissed your instep this morning but you only snorted. It is my sincere opinion that you are the cutest thing going. Have I told you lately that I love you?
>
> Yours sincerely,
> Elvis Presley

I took it out and put it with his papers.

IV Sam, his lawyer father's lawyer son, had made a will. His father had a copy, and I found Sam's copy underneath a stack of canceled checks and some old copies of *Road and Track*. I think he must have told me about it, but making a will for Sam was one of those romantic and secret gestures that has a legal channel in the adult world: he had both sides of the coin at once. He was doing the right thing and acknowledging his wild side at the same time. What a combination of the brave, heroic, protective, restless, and solid.

Two weeks after the funeral, Leonard called and asked me to have lunch with him. That meant serious business. Leonard was not the sort of father-in-law you popped in to have lunch with. You were summoned, casually. I had been to the Baxes' every other day for the past two weeks, and I had spoken to Meridia every day. I talked to my parents every day too, who called from Connecticut. All in all, we tied up quite a lot of lines. There were always people at the Baxes', sitting stiffly in their chairs: Henry Jacobs, the Baxes' friends, tastefully garbed in navy blue and brown, and I felt like a guest too; I was kissed politely and had my hand shaken. I felt they were all angry at Sam for dying. He had created a scene, and I was his accomplice.

My telephone conversations with Meridia were gentle and soft. Neither of us knew whom to be more worried about. To say I was fine would have been a slap in her face. After all, it was *her* son I had lost. I wanted to mourn in a way that would have eased her but I couldn't find it, so we stayed formal. Sometimes at night I had the urge to write her a long letter, a letter that would explain what I felt and how I felt it, but Meridia did not like excess. It was the excessive part of Sam that was the family's trial, after all.

I would lie in bed and think about the conversation we might have if I sent such a letter, the sort of talk you have after you have fallen honestly into someone's arms. She would open up her cut-off secret heart to me. She would say, "I can only love according to my own formula. I love my boys in the way a mother ought. That's how I was brought up to behave. It's the net around me."

But Meridia said things like, "I think you ought to keep your calcium up. It's a natural calm-down. If you're feeling at all frantic, take milk." The fact is, I didn't know what she felt about me. She dispensed with things in a way that would have admirably befitted the head nurse in a cardiology unit. She dealt with me and Sam in the same way she had gotten her boys off to camp, with all the name tags sewn in straight, with the proper number of socks and the required ratio of shorts to jeans. There was a washing machine in the basement of the Little Crab house, and when I thought about Meridia, I often pictured her standing in front of two large wicker baskets, sorting out the dark colors from the light, the light colors from the white. If she could find the proper slot for things, life made sense. If she couldn't find a proper slot, she invented a new slot for those things that didn't fit her sense of order. The hook on which she impaled Sam is that she never knew what she wanted from him. She smiled, but was never pleased. He knew he was pegged, and he kicked against it, but she pegged that too.

Sam's enthusiasms were brief and quite intense. The rock climbing that had sliced his shoulder lasted passionately for six months and then it was the tennis season again. Tennis was a constant in his life, and swimming, but he didn't think much about swimming. He had learned to swim before he walked.

The only music he liked beside the Top Forty—and he said he liked the Top Forty because he liked to drive—was Cuban, and I never found out who had put him on to it or why he craved it so, but if I came home and Sam was on the couch relaxing, it was with a bottle of beer and a Mongo Santamaria record. Then, in a bar, he heard Hank Williams for the first time, and within a week the collected works of Hank Williams were on the record player. This phase lasted just under a month, and then he went back to Mongo Santamaria.

Sam had the attention span of a fly. He didn't land on anything long enough to savor it, but his intensity was enough. He passed. He passed for studious when he was only manic, he passed for athletic, he passed for normal, if it comes to that. The trouble with Sam and Patrick is that they suffered the emotional dislocation that is the result of too much attention and too little love.

For in their way, Leonard and Meridia were a pair of unreconstructed icebergs. If they had been brought to face their coldness, under that gentility and concern, they themselves might have been shocked. They brought up their boys like healthy weeds that grew on their prize lawn, and cut them back at every turn. Sam and Patrick had dentists for their teeth, counselors for their camp, headmasters for their school, doctors for their allergies, and a tennis pro for their backhands. They had a house in Boston and a house in Maine, and they had perfect teeth and manners too. Every facet of their lives was spoken for, except for the way they were. Sam and Patrick had their own spirits, and it was these spirits that didn't make any difference to Leonard and Meridia. There were family conferences about grades, about classes and subjects, about what sort of sailboat to buy; and when they put in the tennis court at Little Crab, the boys had their say about that as well. It was a democratic family: Meridia wanted her boys to function smoothly, the way the chairs and the cars and the washing machines did. The Bax boys knew they were attended to and prized, but they never knew if their parents had any taste for them at all.

Sam's spirit was one of small-time mayhem. It worried Meridia, since it wasn't part of the plan. He burned with reckless energy, while Patrick smoldered inside himself, exclusive and private. In the neat terminology Meridia indulged in, Sam was the doer and Patrick was the observer, except that she didn't much care what it was Sam did or Patrick thought. Patrick did not know a gesture that was not double-edged, but he knew a thing or two about privacy, and if I had had no other cause to admire him I would have loved him for arranging my privacy for me. He knew when I had had it at the Baxes' and he drove me home. He knew the nights on which I wanted company and the nights on which I didn't. He came up to Cambridge on the weekends, and when he went back to New York, I felt I had lost my chevalier. He knew that I would want to go through Sam's things alone, but he knew that I would want him close by. Or he seemed to know: perhaps he just couldn't bear the thought of having his brother so neatly packed away behind his back. He was as hidden as his father, as remote as his mother, and as intense as Sam, in his way. But you had the feeling that Patrick had reflected upon everything in his life. He was private not because he was remote, but because he was cautious.

Underneath those smoothly functioning Bax boys was the undertow of anger, and everything Sam did was done in a state of blind rage. Patrick's privacy was his form of affront—his spirit rebelling against being shortchanged.

Sam loved me in a way that was as close as love could come to his mother's indifference. It was playful, bouncy, it accepted the situation between us without annotations, and without realizing it, he stuck me like a buffer between himself and his parents. He had a wife, and that warded them off. How could he be wild if he was settled? How could he be in trouble if he was married? He might have known these things, but coming from that emotionally monosyllabic household, how could he have had a vocabulary for them?

I loved everything about him. When I met him, I was as game as a goose, and as dumb as they come. But I knew fleetness when I saw it, and defiance, even in its most inarticulate form. All I saw was energy, married to that endearing force of nature. I learned to recognize a form of knife-edge anger I will never possess, and as I watched my husband hack his way through life there was nothing I could do but love him. He was as devoid of passion as Orangeade, because there was nothing in the world he could pit himself against. What he wanted was straight ahead of him, and he picked it up like a windfall apple. But he was graceful, determined, and volatile, and that combination looked a lot like love to me at twenty-one. But I was all wrong for Sam. Sam, Patrick said, needed a conscience, not an appreciator.

Leonard met me at his club, the sort of dark, brown men's club with large leather chairs and dim chandeliers that Old Boys keep alive. The whole place exuded historical wistfulness: you looked for formal portraits of the 1910 soccer team and the tarnished cup from the Henley Regatta, but it wasn't a college club. It was a lawyers' club and, besides a good kitchen, it contained an excellent library for its members.

Leonard was as sober as his club. He kept his gray hair clipped like a putting green, and beneath it you could see the elegant shape of his skull, the same shape his boys had beneath their flopping hair. We sat quietly in the dining room, whose ceilings were so high you felt diminished. The room absorbed sound, so you were afraid to speak above a whisper but tempted to shout to see what sort of echo you would get back. There were some beautifully dressed white-haired men having lunch alone, and some beautifully dressed young men reading the paper, and some couples Leonard and Meridia's age. No one seemed to be talking.

Had we not been fast eaters, the first part of the lunch would have been a misery. Leonard liked an informal, not very personal sort of chat, but we were too closely connected for that. Anything, even something casual, we said would have been intimate. I didn't want to talk to Leonard. In some stubborn, childish way, I wanted to talk to Sam's father, but

Leonard was only Leonard. We concentrated nicely on our menus, made our choices, and wolfed down our broiled fish and salad. Over coffee, we got down to cases.

"You know, Olly, that Sam's grandfather left trusts for Sam and Pat. They both got some money from their grandmothers, so that was added on. According to the provisions in Sam's will, you are the beneficiary of Sam's trust. The actual provision states that it be held for your children, but in the event there were no children, it goes to you. You also get Sam's share of Little Crab. Those are the sixty acres of the hundred and twenty Meridia's mother left to Pat and Sam. You won't be rich, but you'll be nicely provided for."

I said, "Can you make it all over to Patrick?"

"Now, Olly," said Leonard, "I don't think you should make any judgments of that sort now. I just wanted to tell you what's yours, so you won't worry."

"If it's my money, I can make it over to Patrick, can't I?"

"You can do whatever you like, Olly, but I don't think you ought to do anything at this particular time."

Indicating, of course, that I was in no fit state. But I didn't want Sam's money or his sixty acres. How was I supposed to live with it? I did not admire what I thought, but it crossed my mind that I could not fall in love with someone else on Sam's money. I couldn't marry again on Sam's trust. What would I do with Sam's share of Little Crab, except give it over to the Baxes, who would want to pay for it, thus driving me further from them. Or, if I kept it, could I live any of my own life on it? Five years of marriage had entitled me to quarterly statements and checks, courtesy of the late Cyrus Bax, whom I had never known.

"You might consider keeping the money in trust for any children you might have, Olly. You're certain to marry again." He held me in his gaze as he said this, and I looked back into those round brown eyes, those liquid stone walls.

"Why should someone else's kids get Sam's money? Why shouldn't Patrick have it? He deserves it."

Leonard's face was oblong and his teeth were the size and

shape of almonds. There was a strained look in his eye, and I could not be sure whether it was from discussing these painful issues or the possibility that I might make a scene.

"Look, Olly dear, you talk to Patrick about this and see what he tells you. I've discussed this with your father. Talk to him. He's a lawyer too, after all. We all think you ought to let things sit until you get settled. If you're thinking of moving to New York, it might be helpful to you."

He was the soul of kindness and concern. The fact that he had talked to my father about this made me want to stab him. But I only said, "I'll talk to Patrick. This doesn't sit right with me."

"You were Sam's wife," Leonard said. "This is the way he wanted it. You are legally entitled."

He signed for the check and as we walked out he put his hand on my shoulder. It was the only physical contact we ever had.

For a while Patrick spent his weekends in Boston. Most of the time he put up with his parents, but when the house got too full, or they got on his nerves, he stayed in Cambridge with one or another of his college pals. I knew he was putting himself at my disposal, and while it occurred to me that I might be a comfort to him, I did not see how I could reciprocate. Sadness locks you in. All you can see is your own need. To compensate, I made him an elaborate dinner, and then I sat him down.

"I want to talk to you about Sam's will," I said.

"What about it?"

"I want to make Sam's trust over to you."

"I don't want it."

I said, "Listen, Patrick. I never knew your grandfather. He didn't intend for some stranger to have that money, and your grandmother intended to keep Little Crab in the family."

"This is all very noble, Elizabeth, but I don't want it, and you're entitled to it."

"I'm not speaking legally."

"Neither am I," said Patrick. "Besides, you'll need it."

"I have some money of my own, and I can work."

"Look. I'm not going to discuss this at length. You can give it all to the Society for the Prevention of Cruelty to Yellow Vegetables for all I care, but you're a fool to. It'll nourish you, and you earned it."

"Earned it? How did I earn it?"

"Babysitting," said Patrick. "Babysitting for the late Samuel Pattison."

"That's a terrible thing to say," I said.

"Yes, it is. And it's a true thing too. As far as I can see, you saved the only life he had going for him."

And then the subject was closed.

V I wanted everything to be normal. I didn't want to be treated like a piece of antique glass. My own fragility, and everybody else's, was wearing me down. Sam had wanted to leave Cambridge and move to New York, and that's what I wanted, too, even without him. I was afraid that if I made decisions, if I acted, I would be accused of acting out of panic and grief: after all, I was not thought to be myself. But I was myself, and after a month and a half of suspension, tiptoeing back and forth between exhaustion and desire, I stopped caring much what anyone might think. I wanted to do what had to be done and that fell to the details you arrange after you make a decision.

I knew I would be leaving Cambridge from the day Sam was buried, and I knew there would be a certain amount of hell to pay. Who would Danny Sanderson call when he got mournful? Wasn't it up to me to be there when he called? What would the Baxes do without their link to Sam? Patrick had mentioned to them that I might move to New York, so they invited me for dinner to have it made public. By this time I was down to a weekly appearance, and when Meridia called and specified dinner on Friday, I knew I was being called to account.

Life for Leonard and Meridia had assumed its old shape. Leonard was back at his office, Meridia was back at her charities and garden club. We all wore dark colors in the midst of Indian summer and we walked the streets like ordinary citizens, but we knew in our hearts we were singled out by grief and not like everyone else at all.

I knew Meridia and Leonard well enough to know that they would want to see my leaving Cambridge as my escape from the thought of Sam, assuming that every tree and turning caused me pain, but they were only a quarter right. Landscape does not call forth that sort of emotion except in poems, but then, how else did Leonard and Meridia summon up their feelings? Cambridge was only a city Sam and I had lived in. Our apartment was just a dwelling we had shared. It was the fact of Sam, the being of him, that made me want to crack my head against the wall, not the muddy hiking boots in the hall closet, not the half-finished bottle of Cuban rum, or the undeveloped film in his camera, the rocks at Maine, or the shrubs outside.

Leonard, who was a boy scout to the ends of his toenails, probably thought I was moving to complete what Sam had started, as a pledge. The firm of McKeithan, Jarvis, Spain and Pelling had offered him a junior partnership, and they sent me an enormous pot of lilies two days after the funeral. Since I was moving, I gave the lilies to Meridia, who most likely gave them to some less well-heeled member of her garden club. But there was no completion, no pledge. It seemed a sane and sensible way to keep life marching forward.

Little by little, I began to take stock of my possessions and get estimates from moving companies. I read the real estate page of *The New York Times*. Life was coming back to normal, and although I spoke to Meridia less often, we had more communion than we had ever had before.

Their house in Boston had the same rubbed and polished breeziness as the house in Little Crab. Everything Meridia had was old. You could not, for example, imagine her and Leonard starting out as a young married couple. The silver was the Hollander silver from Meridia's great-great-grandmother. The plates were Leonard's grandmother's, and on it went. The housekeeper-cook had been with the family so long you felt she was an heirloom too. But Meridia was modern. She could cook. She could make English plum pudding, cornbread, baked beans, and veal Cordon Bleu. When you watched her cooking in the kitchen, she looked as if she were pushing everything she touched away from her.

Their dinner table sat sixteen in perfect comfort. When Sam and I had gone for dinner, the four of us dotted that immensity like little islands and the stillness of the room made me want to shout down the alley to get the butter passed. We sat—Leonard, Meridia, and I—packed down at one end. I had lost the knack of knowing what to say to them, and since this was business, we weren't going to talk about Sam, our one topic. My heart gave a lurch of relief when Meridia told me that Patrick had flown up for the day on business and would appear in time for coffee.

"Well, Olly, we hear there's a move afoot," said Meridia. "Have you made any definite plans?"

They knew what my plans were, but I sat at their table, good prisoner, and told them I was moving to New York. Meridia knew how to get things as formal as possible.

"And what about an apartment?" she asked. "And will you transfer to Columbia or Juilliard?"

"I'll get a job," I said.

"A job?" said Meridia. "What sort of job?"

"I don't know, but I'll see when I'm settled."

It was rough going, conversationally. We passed the dishes to one another—it was the cook's night out—and our most enthusiastic moments were devoted to who had written and who had telephoned and which of Sam's friends abroad had sent cables. When Patrick arrived, we suppressed sighs of relief. We could ask him how the weather in New York was, and what plane he was taking back. When we had coffee in the living room I was not called upon to talk much, since they had Patrick. And then I realized that with Sam gone, there was no reason for us to be connected at all. There were no grandchildren to bind us together. It seemed to me that I was being written out. Since I was no longer married to Sam, because there was no more Sam, I carried as much weight as a girl who had had a brief affair with their son during a summer of his life.

Meridia's emotional spectrum ran from the polite to the

concerned. Warmth didn't filter through her prism. The friends she and Leonard had were friends of their youth. Their most recent acquaintance had been formed twenty-five years ago. Sam was the impulse behind our connection, and if I had hung around for twenty years and produced some children, I would have been family too. Meridia and Leonard liked to have the reasons for their connections clear and traditional: they did not form friendships of the heart. They formed friendships of the school, of the college, of the club. Then there was family, and they put a large store by family. But I was neither. I was no good to them at all except to remind them of their dead boy. At Christmas we would exchange Christmas cards. When they came to New York for a weekend of theater, they might call me up and take me out for a meal. Sam was what had mattered, and sitting in that lovely room, stirring my coffee with a fancy-backed spoon, I had never felt so ancillary and beside the point in my life. I was being read out of the record. I was being settled in New York. I was no longer Sam's wife, but "the girl Sam was married to." It was not malicious. After all, what good was a daughter-in-law when you have no son? What was binding us now was form, and Meridia was very good at that.

We would have felt awkward if Meridia had admitted awkwardness. It would have done us good to have the conversation come to a startling halt, to have one of us repress a sob or sigh or yawn, for one of us to spill out a sopping, touching story about our absent guest. As it was, I felt we were chattering through clenched teeth. But Meridia knew how to make a conversation go. She spoke as if addressing generalities to an audience of intelligent matrons. Even grief couldn't flatten that. She was talking about air travel, jet lag, and how to take a dog onto a plane: her friends the Ketchams were taking their labrador with them to Brussels. Meridia made you mind your manners. I minded mine, and as I watched her turn from me to Leonard to Patrick, and as I watched us add our parts to the conversation—except for Patrick, who drank his coffee and mumbled as he flipped through a magazine—as I watched her scatter her attention evenly, I felt a rush of anger, like a whiff of pure oxygen. She was being sociable for the benefit of a stranger, and I was it.

But I had my side, too. What good are in-laws if you haven't anyone to be married to? I felt this lost connection keenly, but somewhere in their heartless souls, Leonard and Meridia accepted it as a fact of life and simply acted on it, although they were certainly up for being concerned and helpful. When it was time to go, there were kisses all around.

I offered to drive Patrick to the airport, but he asked me to drive him to Cambridge instead.

"I thought you were taking the last shuttle," I said.

"That's what I thought, but I'm tired and I didn't want to stay with Leonard and Ma."

"Where do you want to stay?"

"I can stay with Danny Sanderson," Patrick said, "but I thought I might put up on your couch. You're my sister-in-law, aren't you?"

I said, "I'm not their daughter-in-law any more."

"Oh, don't let them bother you. Meridia's very limited in her range of feeling and Leonard is a well-intentioned stick. You see the wonderful job they did on their lovely boys, after all."

He was looking straight ahead at the road. With such enigmatic one-liners Patrick interpreted his family to me, but they were only one-liners. The look that went with them seemed dangerous to me. I did not ask for further explanation. I parked the car in front of my apartment house and killed the motor.

I said, "Patrick, will I see you in New York?"

He stared at me abstractly for a moment, wearing on his face the most complicated look I had ever seen: a mixture of scorn, tenderness, impatience, and anger.

"That's not a question that deserves an answer," he said. "No matter how bereft you're feeling."

When I think back on those days, they seem unfocused, as if all the fine edges had been washed out. Grief had put a film over everything—a comfortable blur, it is called.

Patrick and I took the eight o'clock shuttle. It had been decided that I would fly down to New York with him because Sara Lazary had a friend who was getting married and giving up an apartment. I was supposed to meet Sara, but when Patrick called her from La Guardia, she had canceled out, and it was Patrick who took me to the apartment of her departing friend.

Sara's pal was Susie Espinoza, and she lived in a brownstone on Bank Street. The apartment was on the top floor; the living room looked over the street and the bedroom looked over a garden in which two dogwood trees flanked an enormous Chinese urn. The floors were straight pine board, the walls were white. In the living room were bookshelves, a window-seat, and room for the piano. Susie was a tall, suntanned blonde. Her cottony hair curled at the ends, and was kept off her face by two rhinestone barrettes in the shape of stars. In two weeks she was getting married and going to Chile on her honeymoon. She smiled a large, goofy, disorganized smile and took us to the landlady and her husband, who lived in an airy duplex that took up the garden and first floor. Patrick was a witness as I signed the lease. It was a neat transaction. Susie Espinoza was getting married and getting out and I was widowed and was getting in. I took a taxi to the airport and was back in Cambridge in time for dinner.

The plane flew into the beginnings of a sunset, through pink and gray clouds, past formations that looked like stalagmites. In my handbag I had a copy of a lease, the keys to a New York apartment, estimates from the moving company, and a cordial letter from the Harmony Piano Movers of Brookline, Mass. I had two weeks in which to pack, see Henry Jacobs, sit stiffly in the Baxes' living room describing my new view. It was all fixed now. I knew it would be fixed when Patrick and I got out of the taxi on that tree-lined street: it was a proper bijou residence for a proper young person. A sunny kitchen. A bedroom big enough for a bed and a dresser. A bathroom trim enough for a woman with a few cosmetics. A clean dwelling with a certain amount of charm. Taking that apartment was as easy as going to sleep. It fit me somehow, but the whole thing went too fast to leave time to reflect on what part of me it fit. What did the landlady look like? Her name was Mrs. Guinness, and she had given me and Patrick a cup of tea in tall, gritty ironstone mugs. She had said, "If you give a party, give us a couple of days' notice so we can adjust to impending noise." Wide smile, slightly crooked teeth. "Isn't it wonderful to come down from Boston and get an apartment in less than half an hour?" she said. "It only happens to out-of-towners."

It was mine now, and trying to remember what Mrs. Guinness looked like, I fell asleep in my windowseat.

Henry Jacobs lived in an apartment near the Radcliffe dorms. He was in his late sixties and had been a widower for ten years. Both Patrick and Sam had been his students, and he and Leonard had a couple of legal societies in common, so he had become, marginally, close to the family. Leonard respected him and Meridia treated him with the deference she would have given to a dignitary from a remote republic.

His apartment had the deep, faded air of Leonard's club but it was cozy. His taste ran to the baronial and he managed to be neat and cluttered at the same time. There was no shelf that was not dense with books, no wall without gilt-framed etchings, drawings, letters from famous justices, degrees. He liked bronzes and cigars, and his ashtrays were as big as dessert plates—alabaster, marble, and granite, affixed to which were bronze panthers, lions, bears, and lizards. A bronze stag the size of a live rabbit sat on his mantelpiece, and one of his students had rested a cigar across its antlers. He seemed to subscribe to every known periodical, and these were stacked in tidy piles on radiator tops, on benches, and on his long hall table. He had once confessed to me that even the *Police Gazette* had a slot in his reading time. The furniture he liked was small but overstuffed, and his couch was a leather one from the office of a molasses broker of the 1850's. He kept mementos. The students who loved him gave him toys. Between the ashtrays and the magazines were little tin cars and wooden animals whose heads moved if you turned their tails, a pencil sharpener in the shape of a whale, a tiny steam iron, and a plastic clipper ship. Queen Victoria's sitting room had nothing on Henry Jacobs' apartment. Of his cleaning lady he said, "Working for me has given her curatorial training. In my will, I'm leaving her to the Fogg Museum.

"I'm quite happy in my lair," he went on, and I expected to see an owl perched on his curtain rod.

He was a small, stocky man with a massive head of gray hair and a leonine face. He had perfect vision, and when he smiled a light of true impishness came into his direct gray eyes. We had tea in his study. I sat in a striped armchair next to some library steps on rollers. On the table at my elbow was an ashtray with a bronze snake curled on its rim, a Sabbath cup filled with stale cigarettes, and three plastic ducks glued to a round mirror. Henry had fixed a tray—a formal tea, with buttered bread, tea cake, and a tiny vase containing three bachelor buttons.

"I don't often have beautiful girls to tea," he said. "So I like to fuss it up."

We sat back, sipping our tea in silence, and it didn't seem odd to be so mute. Like most encounters I was having these days, I didn't know where to begin and neither did anyone else. I was getting used to a kind of formality that set my teeth on edge. But Henry wasn't everyone else. He was happy to sit there enjoying the afternoon. Finally, he poured me out a second cup of tea and asked me if I had made any plans for myself. I told him that I was going to New York.

"Do you have any reason to go besides the impulse not to stay here?" Henry said.

"It's the right thing to do. It's the next step. I don't want to be in school any more, anyway. I should get a job, so that's what I'll do."

"You know, Olly, this is a time in your life when you can think about yourself. You have a course to follow. One of my delights in having dinner with you and Sam was getting to hear you play the piano. I never thought you took your music seriously enough."

"I've gone as far as I can go," I said. "I'm a talented amateur. That's what all my teachers said. I'm fit to play for cultivated professors of constitutional law, but only good enough for that."

"That's an insult to my cultivated ear," Henry said.

"What I want is a job, but I'm not sure what kind. I've got some money from Sam that I don't want. Patrick won't take it and I can't bear to live on it. I don't want to be set apart by it. If I had my way, I'd set up a scholarship for the most deserving law student with a good backhand."

"Sam would love that," said Henry. "But Sam's dead, and now there's you. I loved Sam, you know. I didn't approve of him, but I affirmed him. I love both of those boys. I've always had my eye on Patrick. He's a serious boy. And I've always had my eye on you. You listen to me and stick with that money for a while and let it help you. When you don't need it any more, I'll help you set up a law school scholarship or anything else you like. When you get to New York, I want you to look up an old friend of mine named Max Price. He teaches at the New York Chamber Music Institute and he's writing a book on chamber music in America. He told me months ago that he needs a researcher. So I've presumed and given him your name and I said you'd call him." He reached into his breast pocket and pulled out an index card on which was written Max Price's home and work addresses, and both telephone numbers. I put it in my pocket and burst into tears I could not explain. Henry handed me a Kleenex as if girls wept daily in his apartment.

When I apologized, he said, "Never be sorry for the way you feel. Old people like me have used up our share of tears, and I'm selfish."

I said, "Everything seems like a formal goodbye at a railroad station."

"My dear girl," said Henry. "We haven't said goodbye. I'm going to watch over your life like a spy, and get weekly reports from my friend Max. Hundreds of students walk through my classes, but I never let go of Sam or Pat, and I won't let go of you. When I come to New York, I'll take you out to

Rumpelmayer's. Grandfather Henry speaks! I want a letter every so often and I want you to look after Patrick. He needs you. And you—you just be you."

He kissed me on the forehead when I left.

VI The days went by negatively, like a countdown. Meridia and Leonard went to Bermuda as they had intended to do before Sam died, to pack some golf into their year. Henry Jacobs began the term. My parents worried because my father had business in Switzerland around which he and my mother had planned a holiday. They didn't want to abandon me, they said. But after a weekend with them in Connecticut, they observed that I did not behave in an odd or fevered manner or slump over my plate in anguish. Several hours of earnest conversation convinced them, and they booked their tickets. Patrick's trips to Boston became less frequent and, finally, he stayed in New York.

The plans and packing, the discussions of costs with the movers and the Harmony Piano Movers, the debris carefully stacked and left for the garbage collector, the letters answered, the thank you notes for flowers and cards of sympathy—these were as weighty as the ripples a light breeze makes on a pond. I came to realize, and I realized things one by one, the way you tell off a rosary, what I was not: I was about not to be a resident of Cambridge. I was not a daughter-in-law. I was not a wife to anyone—I was a widow, a negation in itself. I did not know how widows of twenty-seven behaved, and it seemed to me that the old ritualized mourning period—widow's weeds and no colors for a year—must have been a comfort. But it didn't matter. There was no one to behave for, so I was left to feel for myself. Our friends, Sam's and mine, were so numb and tongue-tied it wouldn't have done much good if I had stopped by for a drink, or if they stopped by for a drink. The life of the party was gone, for one thing. And, for another, if I was chipper it would look forced; if I was quiet I would seem mournful. I did not want my feelings misjudged or misappropriated, and I wanted them not to get in the way; I wanted my feelings to myself. So for the time I had left in Cambridge, I carried myself with the same stiff, awkward brand of dignity drunks have—drunks of the sort who know the meaning and impulse behind their condition and stand by it, realizing that to the rest of the world they are only drunks.

These friends were a nice bunch, but among my negations was the fact that I was disconnecting from them, too. Sam liked to have a pack to run with and his pals were all like him: fleet and filled with energy—all in all, a good set to run with, and that was pretty much what we did. Sam had socialized me, in a way. He took me up on the bouncier side of my nature. The other side, what Sam called my reflective side, my brooding side, he took me up on only when he needed it: Sam was one of the most unconscious people I had ever known. Living with him was like living with a horse. So when he suffered at Meridia's hands and didn't know it but stayed up night after night, puzzled and insomniac, his reflective wife offered her analysis. Sam was a good cure for an overly analytic spirit, and so were his friends. He never reflected on the fact of himself: he simply was.

As I packed and sorted and catalogued, I shifted into a kind of overdrive and assembled my baggage the way a factory worker sorts bolts on an assembly line. It left me free to think, and I thought, with astonishment and bitterness, that I was going to go through the rest of my life without Sam. Sam would not know me when I was thirty-five, or fifty. I might have children he would never know, and they would not be his. Sam, who was the first major decision of my life, would never know what decisions followed.

I thought about the way I did things, and the way Sam did things. Sam liked experiences and he liked them exactly for what they were. He liked going through them, and coming out unscathed. To this end, he had formed a brief alliance with a weekend junkie from Boston University for the sheer thrill of whipping down to New York to see how his pal scored heroin. Sam was horrified by injections, so the offer of bliss his friend made him was never taken up, but he had made the scene. He had prowled through Harlem and the Lower East Side; he had watched the ritual—the belt, the spoon, the dirty candle end. He knew how things were done. He had gone to Nepal for a summer and spent the entire time alone in a country about which he knew next to nothing and whose language he neither spoke nor understood. In a particularly ratty mountain inn, he had been seduced by a milkmaid and later in the day fought off the advances of a sikh who was trekking in the Himalayas. In Rome, a second-rate film star had picked him up and offered to take him to a black mass, but he had gotten pneumonia and ended up in the American Hospital. He had committed the act of rapture in Widener Library as a sophomore with a girl whose name he no longer remembered. He liked to hang around truckers' bars, and he liked hill climbs, drag races, and weekends during which he got two hours of sleep. That energy looked like passion, like daring, but it was only a tame form of rebellion trying to burn itself out. In my bones I knew how difficult he was. I knew without thinking that nothing much mattered to Sam. He was a lawyer. He was a sportsman. I was around. And that added up to life, no questions asked. Sam was not interested in why things worked the way they did.

We were the kind of lovers described in books as healthy young animals. Our mutual delights were swimming, fishing, the Top Forty, and screwing, which was our all-purpose cure for everything—boredom, headache, fatigue, and sadness. We left parties early to nip home to bed. Our television collected dust in a corner. We were great nap addicts, and we liked the comfort of pressed sheets and quilts, although Sam's idea of fantasy heaven was to go at it in a chair lift, and he claimed to have figured out a way to do it. In the country, he liked the thrill of the open air. The cop and flashlight of his adolescent necking days put the proper edge on this thrill, but we were never caught. But there was too much sand on the beach, and too many twigs in the forest, we both agreed; so, basically, we hit the sack.

Our pulses were even, our legs were strong, we had shiny hair and healthy teeth, and years of good food coursing through us. That was as deep as we went at the time, and for all our abounding lust, I have come to think that there was not a scrap of true passion between us. We were too young, too available. We had what we wanted and there was nothing to fight for. You can't miss what you don't know about, so we were happy, natural romantics, and our desires were deep enough, but experience had never put any sharp facets on us.

Under all the grief, I thought of Sam in the way I might have thought of someone I had broken up with in high school. The fact that he was dead caused me quite a lot of internal melodrama, but finality displaces that sort of soppiness, so I thought of Sam as if he were just a terminated relationship, and, as I did, I could see Patrick leaning against the stove the morning after Sam's funeral. He was wearing his white shirt, now rumpled from having spent its night across a chair, and the trousers to his pin-striped suit. He looked like a banker caught at a cheap hotel. His hair flopped over his forehead and he had dark hollows in his face. That was the morning he casually informed me that Sam's death spared me the misery of eventual divorce. Patrick had a real taste for oracular utterance, at least where I was concerned, and I was in the habit of taking him seriously. I thought about the misery of eventual divorce. I thought what a hedonist I had been, grabbing Sam up like an ice-cream soda, how I had enjoyed him without judgment, and how, when he had pained me, I let it slip by because the fact of him contained all present delight. Was that blind love?

I had two letters from Sam or, rather, one letter and one note. He was not much of a writer and we both preferred to rack up enormous telephone bills when we were apart. We did not save the notes we taped to the refrigerator door, or at least Sam didn't, because he never kept letters, not even the letters from his grandfather. I never kept his notes because I had him, an inexhaustible source of one-line notes. The one I found was in the box I kept my letters in, saved in deference to the rush of love it must have caused me:

> Fishface. I went to get my racket restrung and to buy
> the shrimp. You get the wine. Sam the man.

The one letter was written in pencil on graph paper, the result of the only one of Sam's infidelities I ever knew about, although it occurred before we were married. There was no reason for me to know—I was still commuting—except that Sam did so love to stew in his own guilt. When I arrived in Cambridge, the week after it happened, Sam looked like a dog that has been severely kicked. He couldn't eat. He was touchy, tired, and oversolicitous. When I asked what was wrong he lied and said he had been studying too hard, and I knew he was lying. For a day I was racked with the fear that he had decided he didn't love me any more, and I resembled a dog that has been beaten and put out on a strange road alone. Sam when he was guilty avoided your eyes the way a child does. He indulged in this form of silent repentance all weekend, causing me alarm, and when he drove me to the station, he told me that he had slept with a girl called Lyle Crosby, whom he had picked up in a bar.

Lyle Crosby, he explained, was a sort of Harvard Square hangaround, and she had been hanging around for a number of years. Because his memory was short, he didn't remember that he had pointed her out to me as one of the landmarks of town. They had been undergraduates at about the same time, Sam said, and she was the one girl everyone wanted to score with. She was a tall girl with dark-blond hair, the sort of girl fashion never touches. The day she was pointed out to me she was wearing an old, expensive raincoat and a pair of brown suede boots. Her hair was straight and cut into bangs, and she was a type I knew and admired. She was aloof and probably had always been. She smoked Camels or Lucky Strikes and had

52

been to the Sorbonne. Her bones were prominent and when she walked you could see the knobs of her pelvic bones underneath her faded, pressed bluejeans. When it rained, her hair never curled and she could talk with a cigarette tucked into the corner of her mouth. Girls like her had exotic backgrounds. They had spent their childhoods in India or Chile or with the Basques in Montana, and they had special skills: they spoke Hindi, or studied plasma physics, or knew how to take apart a car or play court tennis. Or they had odd, offhand interests. You found them reading the *Morning Telegraph* or *Worker's World* or the *Bulletin of the Atomic Scientists*.

Lyle Crosby looked and would always look like something out of a European movie—the girl in black stockings who appears in a long shot of the railroad station. She strode across Harvard Yard, imperiously scattering the undergraduates whom she probably suffered with existential condescension, knowing that to be seen with her was a badge for them. She had friends and lovers, but no one knew who they were—a strange, Olympian, invisible off-campus crew. Sam said she was in graduate school, but he didn't know what field. It didn't matter: I knew. She was someone's most promising student in post-Hegelian philosophy or Chinese thought. When I thought about her, or girls like her, they seemed timeless and indomitable. You could imagine her conception, but not her birth. There had never been a red, squalling Lyle Crosby: there was only the finished product.

Sam had come out of the library late on a Wednesday night and gone to have a few beers. Lyle Crosby was the only girl Sam had ever seen drinking alone at night, and no one ever bothered her. He had seen her around, they nodded to each other, they sat together, and Sam bought them a couple of rounds. He said he had a motorcycle and that was their topic of conversation. Lyle Crosby knew about motorcycles. He drove her home and walked up the stairs with her. He told me this as we parked in front of the station, slumped over the wheel, staring straight ahead.

I said, "What am I supposed to say?"

"I'm sorry," he said. "Oh, Jesus, I'm sorry. It didn't mean anything at all."

He walked me to the train hanging onto my hand with such intensity it was red when I sat down. I don't remember anything else we said, but on the train, watching the dark towns go by, I thought what it must be like to be Lyle Crosby and the thought of her made me feel young, timid, vulnerable, and about as interesting as a loaf of bread. Then I got angry, then hurt, and when I got off the train, I paused briefly to think what a jerk Sam was to tell me, and how he had used me as he might use Meridia—as heavy mother. Two days later I got the letter on graph paper, a not very long letter telling me how honestly he loved me. The letter was followed by a dozen roses and the roses were followed by Sam, who made it down the Thruway in record time. I sneaked him into my room, where we spent an illegal night, and that was the end of that. Sam knew the value of that hangdog penitence, and he knew that if he whipped himself enough in my presence, I would never have the heart to add to his misery. He immunized me with his own sense of guilt.

The last day I spent in Cambridge was a hot, sullen Sunday. Everything had been arranged: the movers were coming in the morning and I was taking the more fragile baggage with me in the car. The Harmony Piano Movers of Brookline had taken the piano away and would deliver it to New York the next week. By evening everything was packed, and the apartment was so bare you could have skated across the floor.

It was unusually hot for the end of October, and no one seemed to be around. My neighbors were away and the streets were empty. Before I went to bed, I took a sentimental journey. I walked past the Coop, past the bar Sam and I frequented, past a craft shop Sam had bought me a terra-cotta chicken in. I walked through the yard to the Fogg, and on the way back, I saw Lyle Crosby buying a paper at the newsstand in the Square. She was wearing her raincoat, standing with a gray-haired man who had a golf umbrella under his arm. It was startling to see her: a moment in my personal history was confronting me, and she, Lyle Crosby, was as mute as a monument—the building in which you were born or the abandoned house in which you once lived. She didn't know what she meant to me, but there she was and there I was. I could have stood in front of her and told her that I was the recent widow of someone she had gone to bed with randomly six years before. She was Lyle Crosby still. It seemed to me that her life possessed a continuity that mine did not and that if I came back to Cambridge in fifty years I would find her unchanged buying her newspaper at Harvard Square with a gray-haired man. Time did nothing to her: she sailed through it disengaged and untouched. Her life contained no events that changed her or beat her down. How safe and comfortable it seemed to me to be Lyle Crosby, used to yourself, snug in that ageless trenchcoat, secure under that Dutchboy bob.

But I did not grab her arm and inform her that she was heavily entangled in someone else's moment of personal history. I bought a copy of the paper and walked away.

It was hot and breezeless when I got home and the apartment had the neutral, lunar aspect vacant apartments have. It was what the place had looked like when Sam and I had moved in. The boxes were tied up with slip knots, the knots Sam had taught me how to tie. It was devoid of anything. I sat on the bed, and for the first time since Sam's death, I put on the radio. You don't want music in a funeral house, and there are times when music is too eruptive to listen to. But it was my last night in Cambridge, so it didn't matter what I heard.

I wanted to hear Hal Bennett's Greatest Hits. He came on at 11:30 in the evening and Sam swore that Hal and his Hits got him through law school. At one time he wanted to send a photostated copy of his degree to Hal in tribute. Life with Sam began in the morning with Hot Rod's Breakfast in Space and ended with Hal Bennett, late at night. I switched him on. His voice was advertised as a cross between rolling fog and chocolate pudding.

Darlings, this is Hal, your best pal. Your main man, with Hal Bennett's Greatest Hits. I got the sounds to crack your hearts. I'm the man to put tears in your ears. For Shirl and Lester, for Flo and X-Ray, for little Ruthie Hill down at Hubies. For Pancho, from Grace and Floyd. I take requests, at your behests. Hal is sending this out for you, little Darlings. "Forty Nights Without You," that all-time golden gasser by Nairobi Johnson.

Sam could reel it off by heart. Forty nights without you.

PART II

VII My first appearance in public as a widow came three weeks after I was settled in New York. The movers came on time, and within a week, when I looked at the rug on the floor, the quilt on the bed, the neatly hung pictures and the dishes stacked on the shelves, I saw that my apartment was mine alone and that I had created a space that bore no relation to any space I had shared with Sam. The objects were the same, but their arrangement was my arrangement, not a communal one. The trunk of his old clothes was in the back of a closet, since I couldn't bear to throw it out. I also couldn't bear to sell his motorcycle, which was locked in the garage at Little Crab—the same Vincent Black Shadow I had met him on. Danny Sanderson wanted it, I knew, and Patrick said I could have gotten a good price for it, but it was too full of Sam's spirit to sell, and too sacred to give to a muddleheaded roughneck like Danny. It was fitting that it rot in a shed in Maine, sprouting cobwebs, rusting and dying of old age. It had been the seat of a lot of Sam's good times and I didn't want it in anyone else's hands.

The only people who had been in my Bank Street apartment were Patrick and Sara Lazary, paying separate visits, and the Harmony Piano Movers of Brookline, who caused the only snag in my flawless move. They stalled and finally showed up on the afternoon of my first public appearance. The movers were two enormous Irish boys called Mick and Chuck, beefy, ham-handed, with huge chests and big smiles. They sat in the living room and killed a six-pack to cool out from the drive down.

"I'm not looking forward to hauling that mother up three flights," Mick said. "Me and Chuck here figured we might need a hoist, but you've got a nice wide stairway so we'll just take the legs off."

In their huge hands, the piano looked as light as an empty picture frame and they set it down with astonishing gentleness.

"We used to carry our own supplies," Mick said. "A case on ice. Remember that time we took that pipe organ from Boston to that town upstate, Chuckie?"

"Rhinebeck," Chuck said.

"Yeah, Rhinebeck. Treated her like a piece of glass, wrapped her in little blankets and mittens for Chrissake, and all we got was a Coke to split between us. Middle of July, for Chrissake."

"We were sweating buckets," Chuck said. "But then we once moved a harpsichord from Cambridge to Newton and got a seven-course meal and enough Scotch to float a tanker."

I made them a plate of sandwiches and they drank more beer. I asked them if either of them played the piano, since pianos were their line of work.

"Chuck over here plays chopsticks and I play the whore-house piano, excuse the expression."

"Mick would play the drums off key," said Chuck.

Mick took from his pocket a red kerchief the size of a flag and mopped his head with it. Then he went into the kitchen to wash his hands. "You don't want to crummy up the keys," he said.

He sat down, tied the kerchief around his head, and played "Slipping Around," which he sang in a deep, off-key tenor. Then he drank the remains of his beer, set his glass on the floor, and played "You Win Again." It went straight to my heart and I thought I might wail for the sheer hearing of it. It was strange to be on this street, in an apartment so clearly my own, filled with two great grinning boys horsing around the piano and singing out of tune with such gusto it would have wakened the deaf out of silence to hear them. They harmonized on the choruses and they had no idea how sweet it was.

They couldn't have harmonized to save their skins. The whole room smelled of beer, of boyish sweat, and that soapy, wet smell that beer-drinking men have. It was dizzying. They sang "They'll Never Take Her Love from Me," "Honky Tonk Girl," and finished off with "What's Made Milwaukee Famous Has Made a Loser Out of Me."

When that was over, they said it was time to leave and I gave them twenty dollars, which they refused.

"The boss told us about you," Mick said. "You lost your husband and we're not taking any money."

"That has nothing to do with it."

"We're not taking it," Mick said.

I said, "Look, I think you have the wrong idea. My husband died in a sailing accident. He wasn't a hero. You moved my piano and you sang for me, so please take this."

"Nope," Mick said. "It doesn't matter. It doesn't make any difference." He walked down the stairs.

I grabbed Chuck by the arm. "Please, Chuck, he's being silly. Take this and go out and get drunk, will you?"

"Okay," Chuck said. "Micky lost his dad a while back, so he's sensitive. Besides, this job was a real piece of cake."

"It would mean a lot to me if you went out and had a good time on this," I said.

"Okay," said Chuck. "We'll drink to you. Thanks a lot, and you keep your chin up."

I sat on the windowseat and watched them as they drove away. It was getting cooler, and the sun was going down. That lovely boyish scent was still in the room. I closed the lid to the piano since I knew I wouldn't play it for a while. It was the last thing to come from Cambridge. I was all moved in.

That night I met my parents—recently back from Europe— to go to a party in Westchester. They picked me up at the station and seemed mildly surprised that I had the where- withal to take a train. I might have been returning from a perilous trek through Burma from the look of concern and relief they gave me. The party was being given by some old friends of my parents and my reason for being there was mostly to get me out of my apartment and into life. It was not a party I had looked forward to very much, but it pleased my parents to see me. It's always a treat to see the bereft dressed up and looking normal. It turned out to be an extremely dull party, composed half of people my parents' age whom I knew and half of people even older whom I didn't know. I spent most of the evening talking to a lawyer called Ephraim Gottschalk whom my father had known for years. I had met him once or twice and remembered that he had a daughter at Bennington. He looked like a classic matinee idol of the forties with real green eyes and silvery hair. His clothes looked as if he had bought them several hours earlier.

At the end of the party, he offered to drive me back to New York, shook hands with my father, kissed my mother, and told them he would get me home as safe as a tick.

The sky was crisp that night, crisp and frosty, and all the stars were out. We talked along quite happily about one of his cases. He was a nice, stagy man and he told me he was separated from his wife.

I asked him in, quite innocently, for a drink. I thought it was the sort of thing you did for an old pal of your parents who has driven you home from a party. In the name of straight truth, it was not entirely innocent, but my motive was company, not flirtation. It was only ten thirty, so I made a fire in the fireplace and when at one point I stood up to poke a log, he stood up too and took the poker away from me.

"You're a lonely woman," he said. "You're a very brave girl." He cupped my chin with his hand.

"I'm not actually either of those things," I said.

"But you are," he said. "You're too young to bear all this tragedy." Then he said, in a voice of truly shop-worn staginess: "I think I should take you to bed."

For a moment I thought he meant he might tuck me in, but then I saw that his face had gone soft and his eyes were like flints.

"Oh," I said dumbly. "That's very flattering, but it can't be."

"I know. I know," he said. "I think you're frightened by your recent loss. It's a cold world, and I think you've been frostbitten." I stared at him with incredulity: where had he learned to talk that way? And what was I displaying that summoned it up in him?

He said huskily, "I think you're very frightened of me."

At that point, I could have told him that he was old enough to be my father, or that he was a crashing bore, or given him a good old slap, the kind of slap you want to give to a dopey ticket agent at an airline counter. Or I could have taken advantage of what I was beginning to realize was a solid option and burst into tears, making sobbing references to the recent horrors in my life and the cruel hand fate had dealt me. It is not for nothing that boyish piano movers refuse a tip from girlish widows.

But there was Ephraim Gottschalk holding my hands and I could see that he believed, because he wanted to believe, that I wouldn't go to bed with him because he frightened me. You cannot tell a man who has his ego on the line that you don't want him because he doesn't appeal to you. In such instances, the truth is never kind or necessary. It was kinder to agree. He had such a pretty, dotted-Swiss notion of my fear and loss that I let him keep it and I hoped he went home happy with it. After he left I spent a bad half hour wondering if I had somehow been asking for a seduction, but he got what he deserved, and so did I.

My youth and widowhood put me at a slight distance from the world, I realized. My situation gave the impression of virtues I did not feel I possessed, like bravery. I was a brave little girl, or a brave young woman. I felt, in fact, about as heroic as an eggshell, but I was game, and in this world, game looks brave down the line.

I should have known what the world would allow in the way of options, but we primitives are slow to learn, and it was not until Ephraim Gottschalk delivered himself of his set piece that I realized what I could get away with if I wanted to.

These options were useful in times of stress. It is probably easier, and more comprehensible to the world, to act as if your instincts were dictated to you from a greeting card than to know what your natural course is and set out on it. Sentimentality is a second-string emotion, along with jealousy, envy, and righteous indignation. You can assume the second string at will and the world sobs right along with you. It was convenient for the world to assume what I was, since my position should have marked it out, and those piano-moving boys refusing my money touched and angered me for quite a long time.

How dear and innocent I might have been, how mournful and sad. I could have become slightly haggard and my voice gone plaintive. I didn't want any of it. My reactions seemed to me so private that I began to feel there wasn't a place for me in the world at all, and between the Harmony Piano Movers and Ephraim Gottschalk, I learned in one day how important it was to me not to be thought about at all, if I was going to be misunderstood. But I didn't want to be left alone either, so I left myself alone with Patrick when I could, since he was in the same state that I was.

My mother and Meridia, I felt, were waiting for The Big Crack, some identifiably odd piece of behavior, a great outspilling, or Deep Weep. They worried about me, and their telephone bills were printed testaments to it. I worried about them. It was hard on everybody. Patrick didn't seem to be waiting for some emotional tidal wave in me, but rather to see what form it would take.

There is something horrible about available emotions. Overuse cheapens every time. Six months before I dumped poor Eddie Liebereu for Sam, he had discovered a facility in himself for tears and seemed to fall in love with the idea of crying. He told me he was being liberated from his more rigid side, the side that told him men don't cry. I said I had seen men cry on occasion, but then it seemed to me that Eddie was crying quite a lot. Tears welled up in his eyes the way they do in children. After one great bout of weeping, he told me that he was finally in touch with his emotions and that he no longer felt it was unmanly to cry. Thereafter, he wept at the drop of a hat or shoe or ignition key. Otherwise, he was as of old. Even in those excessive college days, when I could indulge in tears by locking my door and putting on the Marvelettes singing "Please Mr. Postman," or the second movement of the second Prokofiev violin concerto, depending on what sort of weep I wanted, I was touched by Eddie and his emotional freedom until I discovered that nothing else about him was any different. He had simply turned into what used to be called a crybaby. Tears in public cost, and even a group of two is public. It seemed to me that you cried in front of people you trusted and that they created a bond. Eddie splattered his trust like fingerpaint in kindergarten, and when I went off with Sam I knew I was right.

Sam never cried, which was probably as bad, except that it had more dignity to it. The one time he did break down it was the real thing. It came at the end of an all-night drunk, after he passed the bar exams. Patrick was there, and Danny Sanderson, with a girl whose name I don't remember, and two classmates of Sam's, John Murphy and Reuben Heifitz. And me, but at about one o'clock in the morning I flaked out and drove home. At seven in the morning, Sam appeared. He looked quite morbid, and I later learned that he had had a bottle of Scotch and several hundred beers. He also looked beaten, bloated, and sick. I was half asleep but I think he must have stayed in the bathroom for an hour. When I got up, he was asleep on the living-room floor with a laundry bag under his head and a pair of gloves over his eyes. I managed to get him off the floor and into bed. His last words, before he passed out, were, "Forgive me."

I spent the morning waiting for him to wake up, thinking that if I had decided to tie one on, I would have informed Sam, hit every bar in town, spent at least fifty dollars in quarters on the jukebox, danced till I dropped, been sick several times, and kept on going. When I had had enough, I would have gotten myself home, kissed my wiry spouse, and passed out. I would have spent the day in my bathrobe, sipping tea and staggering back to normalcy. At the end of the day, I would have had a light and succulent supper and gone to sleep newborn.

When Sam woke up, he was green. I gave him tea and toast and he went back to sleep. Late in the afternoon, he took a shower and appeared wrapped in a big orange towel with his hair slicked down. He sat on the edge of the couch with his head in his hands, and at first I thought he was only getting used to what must have been, or should have been, a massive hangover. When I put my arm around his shoulder, he buried his face against me and began to sob.

"I wish someday you'd tell me how essentially worthless I am," he said. "Why do I do it? Why do I do it?"

"Do what?"

"I get myself sick. I let all my shiftless impulses take over and I never do anything anyone could be proud of."

I reminded him that all he had done was to get drunk, that the cause of the drunk was his passing the bar exam. I told him how much I loved him, and that everything he did made me proud. His eyes were red and he was pouting, but he really was stricken, for all that he looked like a spanked boy.

"Name one thing," he said. "One thing you could be proud of."

"If I were the outside world, I'd say the law review, your senior thesis, and having Henry Jacobs admire you."

He stared at the rug, and when he turned to me the expression in his eyes was truly bitter.

"Those are the stickers on my windshield," he said. "Not the floor I stand on." Then he let himself be comforted, and the next day he was as good as new. He knew what those windshield stickers were worth, but for that one moment, when he forgot, he was desolate.

VIII The first three months in New York, besides getting used to my surroundings, I did almost nothing but think about Sam. I wanted to know what was his part and what was mine. I thought about Patrick coming into the kitchen the morning after the funeral to tell me that I had been spared the misery of eventual divorce. And I did not want to remember, but I did, that at the moment he said it I had known it was true. The more I thought about it, the less I could locate anything, clouded by love and loss.

I kept my time to myself because I needed to. Nothing was going to be normal until I made it so, but since I hadn't, it seemed just and proper to face the chaos, which I knew was finite. So I did not call Henry Jacobs' friend Max Price, although I did write and tell Henry I was putting it off for a few months. I did not call the number of friends who wanted to invite me for dinner and get my life started again, the way you would kick over the engine of a car that has been left out in the cold.

The things I loved Sam for did not need to be romanticized. He had filled the car with roses and bittersweet on our first anniversary and we had driven into the country amidst all those flowers. The weekend he went trekking in the Smoky Mountains with Danny Sanderson, he brought me back a split-oak basket with my initials woven in. He remembered events in our courtship by songs from the Top Forty. He liked to kiss on the street at night.

When I met him, he seemed to me like some bright,

dangerous object on a dark road that you go toward because it shines at you. Up close you see that it is a phosphorescent marker, or a white stone, or a patch of luminescent tape, but before you see what it is, all you see is brightness facing you out of the night, and if you are alone on the road, it is beautiful and frightening.

Sam was my comet. Up close, he was a comet still, but he was the comet I came home to live with. He was bright and dangerous and I knew the alternative to having him was something the world would consider a safe bet, and that was not the sort of safety I was after. I was for the safety that lives on the side of the roughnecks. But that might have driven us apart: Sam only took chances in the world. It was the world against him—the hill climb, the uninsurable motorcycle, the swaying twenty-foot ladder propped unsteadily against a crumbling barn. He took calculated risks. When I met him, I was in love with anything that shoved you out on a creaky limb. As I got older, my notion of risk changed.

Sam was my risk. He was the biggest emotional risk I had ever taken, and it seemed to me that it was in love and friendship that risk is real. A broken bone is a broken bone, but a broken heart is quite another thing. Sam's risks were risks of the bone, and they did drive us apart, since he died as a result of one. His risks were only dares.

Sam's chance on me was in no way like my chance on him. I was a sure thing, surer than the shock absorbers on his Black Shadow, surer than the law boards. I was his cheerful companion, happy bedmate, his introspective, musical, well-placed wife. In my deep appreciation of him, I was nullified. Anything he did was fine with me if he was doing it, and I believed that if you loved, you loved uncritically. If I had taken exception to Sam's ways, how could I have loved him at all? It would have canceled everything out. I knew what I had married, and I stuck by it.

But to Sam, I was only a sure thing. I was the wedge he stuck between himself and everything else. I was his lead line to an emotional world where he took no chances at all.

I thought of him in that fragile Sailfish, watching the storm blow in. I could see him grinning, calculating himself and the boat against it. He was probably having the time of his life when he died, and it probably never occurred to him that Patrick and I might be heartsick. The Bax boys tested themselves constantly, and in those times there was never anybody else, only themselves and their nerves. When I thought of Sam in that boat, a wave of anger swept me and I let it sweep. I saw myself standing completely useless watching his brother watching him. How outside it all I was! What sort of a woman was I to let my husband, the love of my life, die by making a damned fool out of himself? I did beg him not to go, so I had done my part, and he had looked petulant and stubborn when I tried to stop him. There wasn't any stopping him. His whole life was like a traffic accident that I was witness to. I watched it to the end, always about to but never quite standing in its way.

When I looked back on our beginning, I saw a long-legged girl, with dark, shiny curly hair standing on the road wearing a proper Chesterfield coat with the collar turned up, confronted by a wild person on a huge bike. Standing in back of him, crash helmet in hand, was his nice stolid pal, his tame rider, my beau, Eddie Liebereu. That dark-haired girl surveyed the two of them and knew at once she was standing on the wrong side, that all her impulses all her life—every acceleration on every curve, every gallop without a saddle, a scrapbook filled with yellowing pictures of James Dean, every joy ride—put her with that grinning Bax, that dangerous, accident-prone kid, that hero. It was not for nothing that "He's a Rebel" by the Crystals was on the college bar's jukebox for two years and it was not in vain that I fed my dimes to it. To have your rebel be second in his class, to marry your rebel, to have your rebel make law review buttered both sides of the bread and coated it with strawberry jam. What a life it was.

His part was that he never could sit still, and my part was that I watched him with such deep pleasure. The recklessness in my nature was quiescent, and I thought that anyone who did not view Sam or anyone like him with admiration was half dead, or all dead, or lying.

On our third anniversary, Sam took me to a boxing match. It was held in a gym in the south end of Boston where local fights were held. You sat on camp chairs, and brought your whiskey in a paper bag. The place was filled with truckers, longshoremen, nightwatchmen, and bookies. I had never seen so many massive shoulders in one place. We sat down to watch Kenny Reilly take on Josco Pierpont of Montreal, and there was a nice, mellow aura in the place. When the fight started, something changed. The tension mounted until you felt the gym was boobytrapped with live wires. Sam said there were always fights after fights and when Josco Pierpont knocked out Kenny Reilly, the Boston Wonder, all hell broke loose in one intense corner of the room. A couple of bottles smashed against the wall, a camp chair was thrown into the ring. A couple of drunks were going at it.

Sam shouted, "Put the chair over your head!" And when I looked at my boy wonder, his eyes were shining. It was just the sort of thing he loved: violence and protection. He moved us through the crowd and got us out before the police moved in.

In the car he said, "That wasn't a real blowout. Patrick and I once saw Sugar Ray fight and they threw bottles from the top tier."

That fight held me for a long time. At night, I dreamed it in slow motion. I remembered the flat band of blue smoke above the ring, the feeling of heat and restlessness before the fight began. The air was so charged you thought a lit match would cause an explosion. But for Sam it was only another fight: it hadn't been a big blowout after all.

There was no one I could clear this all with, no one I wanted to talk to. There was Patrick, but together we behaved like a pair of survivors of a dreadful shipwreck who want each other's company as a memento of the experience, but not for a dialogue about it. Patrick was around a lot those first few months. We went to the movies. We had dinner. He helped me put up bookshelves, and we went for walks. When Patrick didn't want to talk, he was the man who invented silence. Sam had been private by default: he didn't know anything about himself, so there was nothing for him to reveal—he liked things to be revealed to him. With Patrick you felt he knew everything about himself but would only tell you what he wanted when he felt like it.

Then there was Sara Lazary. She was either the most private or the most evasive person I had ever known. Talking to her was like talking to a stranger uncertain of the language or the culture she found herself in, but it was all by design. She was very clear and glossy. Her hair was honey-colored and her eyelashes were jet black. Her eyes were brown, and they always seemed downcast, as if she had a book on her lap she was reading in secret while she talked to you.

Once in a while, she turned up and we went out to lunch. She never spoke about Patrick. He mentioned her, but not often. When you saw them separately, they seemed to have no connection at all, and in the old days when they appeared together, I was always amazed. Whatever communion they had between them seemed so special I could not imagine them making plans or discussing anything as ordinary as where they would meet. To me, they were an established fact of life—Patrick and Sara—but I didn't know a thing about them. Did she call him at work? Did he cry on her shoulder? Did they spend weekday nights together? Their silence about each other seemed so enforced I couldn't ask. Asking would be blundering and so I assumed they had some transcendental, secret, uncrushable bond that made references in front of a third party entirely unnecessary.

Her style was so particular it made you feel you knew something about her. Everything she wore looked like the only one of its kind: her skirts were embroidered, her blouses were monogrammed, her sweaters were crocheted, and her shoes from year to year were the sort of shoes you thought they weren't making any more. If you asked her where she got any of her clothing, she would tell you the name of the shop and how many years ago it had gone out of business. She was immaculate and nothing she owned was new; her touch on things was so light it looked as if everything she had would last forever. Her handbags were always black, and everything inside them was green. She had a green wallet, a green checkbook, and a green cigarette case. When she spoke, you felt she had considered her every sentence for a long, long time before she made it public, and she never made mistakes of fact. Her profession, as much profession as she had, was translating from the French, and a large part of my conversation with her concerned musical references in whatever she was working on. I spent several afternoons with her and never mentioned Sam or Patrick, although I wanted to. She seemed to accept the way things were without reflection.

When she was gone, I thought about the shape her life appeared to have and it looked as clear as glass and as shapely as a Brancusi statue. She would not have married someone like Sam. If she had, she would not have allowed him to die. I imagined her sitting at a rosewood desk, working on a translation with a gold-tipped fountain pen. She was another Lyle Crosby. Nothing about Patrick would break her heart, but she didn't seem heartless, only contained, only level— someone with a fixed mind and no holes in her life. In her unswerving correctness and by her unflappable elegance, she made me aware of a curious sideproduct of tragedy: embarrassment. Grief and mourning single you out. You are the one afflicted, while the rest of the world goes off scot-free, even if you know that death catches up with everyone. If you are recovering from the death of someone near you, you are its victim: it happened to you, and not to anyone else.

Sara probably wasn't unsympathetic. If she had talked to me about Sam, she might have been a comfort. But even if she had, she would have been a representative of the healthy, untouched world, needing to console one of its stricken former members. Her surface looked so unshaky, so contained, that even though I sat in my corner of the world, in my chaste and charming flat, I felt that I wore sackcloth and jabbered out of politesse in the face of disaster. Sara was like a visiting nurse, or so I saw her. It would have been more fitting if I had been a wreck, but my hair was properly cut, my clothes were crisp and fitting, and when I looked in the mirror I saw only a slightly tired edition of my same old self.

Sara got me out of doors. We went to the Frick and to an exhibition of Gerard David at the Metropolitan. As we walked those polished halls and corridors, we looked like serious girls doing some comparative study, except to me. I was being dragged around, but Sara was effortless. Our conversations were the conversations of a pair of blue-stockings, and my impulse to sit her down to lunch and blurt Sam's name or Patrick's withered in the face of her stalwart avoidance. A day with Sara left me tired of trying. It was my fault, not hers.

After a few of these expeditions, I began to wonder if there was a space in Sara's life that I invaded, something that had to do with the notion of death, or something between her and Patrick. Perhaps she was merely being polite, taking someone's sister-in-law out for an airing. It could have been that the death of Sam—of anyone—was terrifying. Or she simply had nothing to say about the matter. Or she wasn't interested. But she seemed to me like an egg, a perfect, opaque oval with no edges, that will crack at any point or at no point at all.

IX In December, Patrick took me to a coffee concert. This was one of a series of chamber music concerts given by the Society for Stringed Instruments, which resided in an old brownstone off Madison Avenue. You walked into a formal, mirrored room, in the center of which was a small stage. Clustered around it were a series of tables laid with white cloths. On each table were a brass samovar and plates of Danish pastry. The idea was to listen to music in perfect comfort, having polished off your Danish and coffee before it started.

It was cold, and snowing. Patrick picked me up and when I gave him a drink, he said, "Don't you think it's a little old-fashioned to wear black all the time?"

"I don't wear black all the time."

He said, "Every time I see you, you have on at least one black garment."

"I don't feel like wearing colors yet," I said.

"I had no idea you were so theatrical," Patrick said. "Besides, our Sam would probably approve if you were racing around in yellow."

"I wouldn't like it."

"I don't think you ought to put yourself at such a remove."

I told him I didn't think I was living at such a remove, but it wasn't true. The delivery boy from the grocery store, the man who owned the dry cleaners, Mrs. Pratt in the stationery store didn't think I was at a remove. I smiled and nodded. I spent afternoons with the selective Sara Lazary, nodding and smiling. I knew I was living in a sling, but what could I do? My energy had abandoned me and I was living in a state I could not approve of. I was unenthusiastic, quiet, craving solitude and enfeebled by it. I was learning what distance was all about, and I was perpetuating it. I didn't want the start of a new life; I wanted to get used to things slowly. So I had not set out on any course, and although I was living on my own funds, Sam's were locked away and that padding frightened me. I thought I would know when my spunk returned, and then I thought I would have to summon it. It was as if every feeling I had ever had was crowding me in one great swoop and there was no way for me to fix on anything at all.

We were quiet on the drive uptown. At the door of the Society for Stringed Instruments, Patrick took my coat, and when he had checked our coats, umbrella, and scarves, he took my arm and we walked down the hall together. He had gotten the tickets from one of the partners in his firm and we were the youngest couple there. We were poured cups of coffee, and while we passed the cream and sugar, the members of the Manhattan String Quartet came in and took their places on the stage. A printed card announced the program: Brahms Quartet in C minor, the Haydn Quartet in A, and Beethoven's Harp Quartet. It was the first music I had heard since Sam's death, with the exception of the Harmony Piano Movers and fifteen minutes of Hal Bennett, but I wasn't overwhelmed. He wasn't there at all. You could have gotten Sam to a coffee concert as easily as you could have gotten a garter snake to eat a brick, and if by some massive coercion you did get him to go, you had to be afraid of what he might do once he was there.

I sat back in my armchair, happy enough in that darkened room, wearing my chic and useful black dress. It was short-sleeved, and my bare arm touched the arm of my properly suited brother-in-law. It had been a long time since I had looked at him unfettered—as another person, not a part of Sam's family. He looked a little like Sam, but his hair was darker, his eyes were pure hazel, and his features were less round. He didn't sit like Sam. Sam sat on the edge of his chair.

Patrick sat back deep with his legs stretched in front of him as if he were settling in for a leisurely julep or an afternoon nap. As I watched him, a feeling of deep camaraderie took me over, and by the time the Harp Quartet came around, I had a strong desire to hold his hand.

On the way out, he took my arm, as a proper escort would. The streets were icy and we stood under a streetlight waiting for a taxi, watching the snow flurry. We sat close together in the cab and I leaned my head back to watch the snow. I was suddenly happy in my coat, happy from the music, happy with the coffee and pastry, and what part Patrick had in all this I didn't know. I was glad he was there, with me, and in that taxi cab that snowy night, with Patrick next to me, I passed through some point in my own mourning, or maybe I had outlasted one of grief's metabolic cycles.

Patrick said, "Did you call Henry's friend yet?"

"Was this concert a set-up for that question?"

"Only marginally," he said.

"I'm going to call him tomorrow. I haven't felt like it, but I do now." I leaned back, feeling as invalids do when they sense their strength returning.

I said, "Patrick, I've been very self-centered since this happened."

"We all are," he said.

"But you aren't."

"That's what you think, because you're stuck inside your own skin at the moment, so you only react. We're both very prideful, so don't worry about being a comfort, or getting comforted."

He walked me up the stairs, and while I made a pot of tea, he built a fire. I watched him from the doorway and on his face was a look I had never seen before. It was his equivalent of Sam's blank stare, the stare he summoned up before he went out for a kill on the tennis court. Patrick looked ready to take the poker and wreck my wall. The hold he had on himself looked as if it were strangling him. You never saw that on Sam; he was so much himself there was never anything to fight. But

Patrick looked about to break out of something, something very deep. It wasn't frightening, but to see him made my knees buckle slightly.

When I came in, he put the poker down and began to pace. Then he stopped, faced me, and put his hands on my shoulders.

"I hope you know what you're doing," he said.

"You mean now, or in my life?"

"All the time," he said. "All the time."

"I always know what I'm doing," I said.

He let go, and turned away. Whatever was on his mind, he had managed to create enough electricity to make me shake. It was pointless to ask him what process he was going through. You learned that Patrick always knew what he was about. When he wanted you to know, he would tell you. He and Sara, I imagined, had a dark, intuitive bond, something deep, indirect, and particular.

There is a difference between privacy and dignity, but they look like the same thing. Living with Sam had made me pretty direct, and I was forthright to begin with. You had to be direct with Sam, and that's all he had wanted me to be. When I realized what could be surmised about me just by my being a widow, I felt my privacy invaded, but it was only my sense of dignity. As soon as I stopped putting myself at a remove, the world would move in, with all of its conceptions and misconceptions. In some way, with this undeniable label on me, I wasn't free. I wanted to keep private except from what I chose. The difference between me and Patrick was that he wanted to keep private from everyone. My widowhood was my edge, the thing that set me off from other people, or so I felt. Patrick and Sara, for that matter, had no edge to offer. They didn't even distinguish themselves as a couple.

You couldn't ask Patrick what he meant, in the same way you couldn't ask Sam not to go sailing in a storm. That flint-headed stubbornness ran in both of them, but in Patrick it had more purpose. Patrick was cautious. He was smart enough to know what he protected, while his younger, bat-headed brother squandered himself to death.

When Patrick left, I straightened up. I washed the teacups, swept the hearth, and banked the embers. Without him the place seemed emptier, and I lay back on the sofa and lit myself a cigarette. I stuck two of Meridia's needlepoint pillows in back of my head, kicked off my shoes, and put my feet up. I smoked and watched the snow come down. I didn't think about Sam or Patrick. I thought about me, lying in my chic and useful black dress, stretched out on a long sofa smoking a cigarette. I was a twenty-seven-year-old widow, but as I watched the snow slant against the window, I thought: There's more life. Grief is what the body goes through to get over grief. I needed my solitude to expend it, and I thought that if I had gone out in public with it, I would have gone into the world a fraud: it was too easy.

But there was more life. The official part of my life with Sam was over, by horrible accident, and my months of getting used to it were upon me. I yawned and stretched, and it seemed to me that I had passed the end of what Patrick called my "remove." I could feel the couch cushions under me and the pillows propping up my head. How delicious the cigarette tasted, and how eerie and quiet the street was in the snow. When I looked around my living room, I felt like someone writing the book of Genesis: I had created it and it was good. The remains of the fire blinked red from the grate. The hearth brush, the Cape Cod lighter, the two gilt angels on the fireplace, the rug on the floor gleamed too. I saw that without much effort I had made a place for myself without Sam, which Sam would never see, a cozy, comforting sort of a place, a place there would be more life in. The phrase "there's more life" went through my head like the song your neighbor down the hall plays over and over. No one ever tells you that grief takes over your body, and as I lay there watching the light shine on my stockinged legs, I realized I was recovering. I was beginning to savor my own life.

Or as I had savored Sam, The More Life Kid. I had been his admiring accomplice, his ardent sidekick, his loving appreciator. I appreciated him the way I appreciated everything, in an intense, lazy way. Somewhere along the line, Sam must have known that, the way he came to know anything useful to himself: he used it. You have to perform an ax murder to alienate a steadfast appreciator, and since Sam never did murder, anything went.

When we met, we went off like a pair of sparklers. We did not connive for one another, but were casual as Lake Michigan fishermen when the smelt are running—we were that available. I did not spend time wondering if Sam would come through, since that wasn't what I wanted him for. I wanted him for his presence, which in the end is more frightening than wanting something specific, like less horsing around on a 1500cc motorcycle with no insurance, more punctuality, or more self-appraisal. I wanted him to be, in one great gulp, and when he was around, I was a happy human. Since the moment his death had been verified, not one day had passed without my wondering if I could have saved him if only I had wanted more, if I had made my claim and done some limit-setting, if I had not been so fixed in my belief that you cannot tamper with the one you love. It occurred to me that Sam had buffaloed me into a state in which I had no demands, since he was my only demand and that had been met. Sam wasn't perfection, but he was good enough for me and whatever he did that drove Meridia and Leonard up the wall, that was okay too. Besides, I was his right-hand man.

What you wanted to do with Sam was grab him and go dancing. That's what he was good for. He was good for great bursts of unquestioned joy. The best thing about him was that he took things as he found them or as they came to him. It was the worst thing about him, too, since one of the things he took as he found was himself, and then me. I was his other half, the pensive wife who explained what he couldn't see. He liked to have things explained to him in the bathtub, generally speaking. Things made more sense to him, he said, when he was submerged in warm water, and with their dry knees sticking out like islands amongst the bubbles, Sam Bax and the former Elizabeth Olive Marcus talked things over. But there were no complaints on either side, because I was just fine with him too. He really loved me, Sam did, in a way most people don't get around to unless they are close to sainthood; he gave out a kind of disembodied, all-accepting love. In Sam's case, it was probably the result of not caring very much. If you loved someone, you loved, and that was that. There was no reason to implement what was established fact.

At twenty, and at twenty-seven, my heart was the heart of a teenager—overexcited, overstimulated, and very devout. The teenage heart teaches us that to alter one part of the one you love is to falsify love entirely. In college, I used to sit around with my roommate, a girl from Livermore, Ohio, named Rosie Stone, and pass the time in emotional speculation: if the one you loved loved someone else, would you aid and abet him in his love? If the one you loved wanted something you didn't approve of, would you help him get it? If the one you loved sincerely wanted to go away, would you let him? Help him? To these questions Rosie and I, wide-eyed and moronic at eighteen, gave a solid, heartrending Yes. Love was the only thing we gave any credit to: the life of the emotions was what kept the body going. At eighteen, walking around and throbbing with these beliefs, I was what Thomas Hardy said Tess of the D'Urbervilles was: a vessel of emotion untinctured by experience. What did I know? I wore my mother's old hacking jacket in the fall, and a shredding Chesterfield I held onto for sentimental reasons in the winter, and walked waiflike around the campus feeding my rich young heart. At twenty-seven, I had conducted several love affairs. I had, in the name of love, been ruthless and cruel to a perfectly acceptable wimp named Eddie Liebereu. I had married my own true love and lived by his side for five years, and now I was someone's accomplished, widowed sister-in-law. But under my polished limbs, under my hair, I was a grubby little teener sitting in my room listening fervently to The Four Seasons singing "Big

Girls Don't Cry" when I was not sobbing to the music of Gustav Mahler. I kept a notebook full of adolescent compositions my father referred to as "that goddamned cubist music" and brooded about Lili Boulanger, who wrote a mass and died young. I was one short step away from the even grubbier eleven-year-old who thought the world ended when Donald Turnipseed ran down James Dean in California.

I had spent my life refining what I felt, and Sam was the object I had chosen to reflect on, forever, I thought. I was not far away from me and Rosie Stone talking all night about our emotional instincts. We were in the process of refining, and once that starts, it never stops. What Sam did was just live.

When I got off the sofa, I stretched my bones, drew the curtains, and went to bed. It was no accident that it was the first night I did not find myself in the grip of painful tears and it was no accident that the first thing I did in the morning, after a peaceful cup of coffee, was to call Max Price, the friend of Henry Jacobs, the professor of our Sam, our lovely boy.

X Max Price met me for lunch at a tearoom near the Museum of Modern Art. When I asked him on the telephone how I would recognize him, he said: "You'll know me. I look just like Henry except I'll be wearing a loud green tie."

The tie in question was lurid emerald green—you could have seen it in a cave. The rest of him was perfectly sober, and he did look like Henry Jacobs, whom he had known all his life. They were the same general size and shape—small and leonine—and the lines in their faces came from thought and sorrow, not from tension and confusion. His wife taught Russian at a Sacred Heart College and was responsible for the lurid tie.

"She started buying these horrors for me when we were young," he said. "She said I was the oldest person in the world and that she had always wanted to be married to a visible eccentric. Last year, my son sent me a yellow tie with a hula girl embroidered on it."

He wore a gray suit and a watch chain, and he was not at all formal. We had Henry in common, and Henry believed that when two strangers meet through a third person whom they both love, nothing can go wrong. Over lunch, we discussed my job. What he wanted was a researcher for his book on American chamber music. He wanted reviews of first performances, letters to and from composers.

"Does it sound dull?" he asked. "You'll be sitting in libraries quite a lot, but Henry thought it might be something you'd find useful for a while."

I said, "Henry thinks I should have an interim."

"Do you think so?"

"I've had my interim. I've been sitting around for four months."

He looked at me with a kind of apersonal tenderness.

"Four months isn't a very long time in these situations," he said.

"It's a very long time, if you're me. I'm beginning to feel slack and self-indulgent. I shouldn't have sat around at all except that I get so tired."

Then he smiled. "You kids are so stupid. But, okay. I'm going to put you to work ransacking the Sprague Collection. That's a fat bequest to Butler Library, so I'll call Columbia today and get you a pass and stack privileges."

We shook hands on it, and then I went to have a ramble around the Museum of Modern Art. I ended up having coffee in the cafeteria, staring out the window. It had started to rain and the little patches of snow in the sculpture garden were dark gray and melting. There was a couple hanging around Henry Moore's "Family," a girl in a coat that seemed to be made out of a Navajo blanket and a boy with a hunting jacket. He gave a considered bang to the back of the statue, as if to get an idea of its heft. The girl sat on the base, and then they chased each other around. By this time it was raining hard, and both of them were hatless. The girl had red-blond hair in long braids, and when she spun around they stood out like wind socks. When they were fairly soaked, they locked arms and scampered up the steps. It was gray in the garden, the sky was gray, and the only two points of color had gone. From my seat at the window, they had looked so innocent, living out a moment in time without even knowing it. I wondered if they were lovers who went home to the same home, or a pair of high school students cutting class. It seemed unfair of them to lark away like that, leaving me with the memory of seeing them. They hadn't seen me, but they were in my memory for life, and it occurred to me that, at a certain point, memory begins to be a burden.

Two days later, Max gave me my pass to Butler Library and I started ransacking Mrs. Sprague's bequest. I liked being around Columbia. My own college days had been spent in a bucolic well, the well in the fairy tale that the good sister falls into and then gets covered with gold coins in. Columbia wasn't as enchanted as my college, but the Barnard dorms were probably filled with girls as innocent and mawkish as I once was. Sitting at my little table in the stacks with the desk lamp shining dimly on a bunch of yellowing letters, I thought of the square of the world I was sitting in and what it contained.

In my senior year of high school I fell in love, in an intense, brief, and painful way, with a Columbia boy called Teddy Meecham. He was on his way to becoming a drunk—he wanted to be a drunk when he grew up, like Dylan Thomas— and was probably a jerk, but I saved a memento of everything that ever happened to us. I kept a napkin he wrote a poem on, a parking sticker from the Bronx Zoo, a shoelace, or part of one from the work shoes he affected, and an orange lollipop, which by the time I got around to throwing it out was smashed and matted and quite disgusting. There were probably dormitory rooms filled with junk like that, like Teddy Meecham's name tape, and a warped copy of Garnet Mims and the Enchanters singing "A Little Bit of Soap." I thought there must be thousands of letters, tied up with ribbons or rubber bands, hoarded all over campus. Those unknown lovers at Columbia were as remote to me as Teddy Meecham: it was the first time I had thought about him in years, but I suddenly remembered how I had felt about him, the way I brooded over those souvenirs of his being, cried over his incoherent letters, which I carried with me wherever I went, and the longing they dredged up in me. I wondered about him and about Sam, one gone and unknown, the other just gone. I wondered if the love I bore had been in vain, and how much vain loving was being generated as I sat in my dark corner of the stacks. As I thought about it, I made my notes on three-by-five cards. The light from the desk lamp was the shape of a cone and I was surrounded by a deep, dusty, leathery smell. It was a close, private place to think and I wondered if there might not be

84

some overheated undergraduate sitting several stacks down writing heartfelt prose to his girlfriend at the University of Wisconsin.

I worked up a real affection for my spot in the stacks and a comfortable affection for Butler Library. When you walked up one staircase, you came face to face with an oversized portrait of Nicholas Murray Butler; you walked up another and got Dwight David Eisenhower, and you also got a large painting of King George and the Queen Mother being handed diplomas. The lady in the coatcheck room and I had a running conversation about the proper way to store wet umbrellas. It was nice work, too. I read about music all day.

On a very cold Monday, I came out of the stacks and saw at the reference table an old friend of Sam's named Johnny Porter. He was tall and skinny, and had bright-orange hair. He had been in Sam's class at college and had put in a little time at graduate school, so we used to see him from time to time. Last seen three years before, he had married a girl called Maria, a big girl with wide shoulders, given to wearing capes. I saw him, and my heart failed. I didn't want to see him at all. If he didn't know that Sam was dead, I didn't want to tell him. If he did know, I didn't want to hear whatever he would come up with to say about it. But he saw me, and gave me a smile so shy and tentative, a smile that would have allowed me to smile back and disappear, that I walked over to him.

"Gee, Olly," he said. "I haven't seen you in so long. I just don't know what to say. I thought about writing to you, but I just didn't know how."

I said it was okay, and asked him what he was doing in the library. He took me to the local bar, and over lunch he told me that he was working for a magazine and was checking some references for an article. I asked after Maria, and he said, "We've separated, for the time being." He told me how much Sam had meant to him and asked about Patrick and Danny Sanderson. He asked me if I wanted company, and when I said I did, he put my telephone number and address in a leather book. We parted, and I went back to the stacks.

But instead of researching for Max Price, I found a

biography of Sir Thomas Wyatt and browsed it under the insufficient light. I wasn't reading it very hard until I found a passage about Sir Henry Wyatt, Thomas' father, who was having a fight over his allegiance to Henry Tudor after being tortured by Richard III.

> "Wyatt," said the Tyrant. "Why art thou such a fool?
> Thou servest for moonshine in the water. Thy master is a
> beggarly fugitive. Forsake him and become mine. I can
> reward thee, and I swear unto thee I will."

> "Sir," was his answer, "if I had first chosen you for my
> master, thus faithful would I have been to you if you had
> needed it, but the Earl, poor and unhappy though he be,
> is my master. No discouragement or allurement shall ever
> drive or draw me from him, by God's grace."

I read it over and over, and wrote it down on one of my three-by-five cards. I didn't know why it struck me until I was out in the sullen winter air, walking to the subway. I thought about Johnny Porter telling me that he and Maria were apart. "Dislocation of affection" was the term he used. Sir Henry Wyatt knew that loyalty loved above judgment, and it was loyalty that was your master, not the man. Johnny Porter wore a striped shirt, a blue tie, and a tweed jacket, but he had the kind of body clothes look they are about to slide off of. In fact, he looked very tenuous. I wondered what it was like to undergo a dislocation of affection, and thought how easily some connections are broken in the world of love.

A week later he called me from a bar near my apartment and asked me if I would come and have a drink with him and a journalist called Carlos Warren. It was late in the afternoon, and it occurred to me to say no, but I said yes, put on my coat, and walked three blocks to a local bar, Natty's, which was a hangout for people Johnny described as "Greenwich Village intellectual thugs," but there were only a middle-aged woman who sat at the bar with her Chihuahua on her lap, a man in work clothes chatting with the bartender, and a youthful couple, clearly students, their spiral notebooks stacked in front of them. And Johnny Porter and Carlos Warren.

Natty's was an old bar. The wood paneling was stained black with age and the old-fashioned tin ceiling was black too. The lights were bar lights: beer signs that blinked blue and red and green, a Mr. Peanut lamp, a big illuminated clock that bore the name of a distillery; but the place looked blue in general, and Johnny and his comrade looked as if they had spent the better part of the afternoon getting coated by the atmosphere.

Johnny Porter gave meaning to the term "boiled." He looked as if he had been floating in hot water and then dried. His shirtsleeves were wrinkled from being rolled and unrolled. His jacket sagged limply off the back of his chair and his tie looked soft in the way of wilted vegetables. While I sat there and he got even drunker, his clothes seemed to disintegrate but his jaw tightened, until everything he said came out in a terse, clipped whisper.

But when I arrived, he was only moderately drunk, and he introduced me formally to Carlos Warren, who he said was a war correspondent, just back from the Middle East. Carlos Warren appeared to be sober, but you learned that excessive drunkenness didn't change him at all. He wore a sharp blue blazer, gray flannels, and a French silk tie printed with water lilies. His hair was as sleek and rich as fur, and he wore horn-rimmed glasses. He was immaculate and unruffled, and he was killingly good-looking. He was a magazine ad for a war correspondent. As he got drunker, he became more immaculate. I discovered hours later that it was his affliction to drink himself into a state of rigid, glacial sobriety.

I didn't have much to say for myself, but the two of them took care of that by having a conversation around me. Carlos was talking about Prague, where he had put in a little time.

He said, "You don't understand human scale until you see an unarmed student standing next to a tank. People think New

York is inhumane because of all the skyscrapers, but that's not one to one. When you're up against a tank, you know what's fucking what. The most obscene and violent thing I ever saw was this big Czech kid standing next to a Russian tank. It was just parked on the street. You couldn't tell if anyone was in it, but the sight of a tank is truly gut-crunching. First it looks like an abandoned building, then it looks completely lethal and unstoppable. The kid was looking at it in *awe*. Not anger, not fear, just complete fucking awe."

Then he took a sip of his drink with the same controlled gestures cats have when licking their paws. Johnny looked about to melt. A lot of hero worship was emanating from his side of the table, and Carlos Warren was not catlike for nothing. He knew who the center of the universe was, and he divided his attention equitably, half his gaze to Johnny, half to me, as he went on to tell us about the teenage girl who ran into the square and put a flower on the tank, and what she wore, and how she looked. When he finished, I felt we should applaud. As I looked at him, I saw the flicker of a satisfied smile run across his perfect lips, but behind his glasses, his eyes were as blue as slate and about as hard.

The barmaid brought another round of drinks, which Johnny said was their tenth, but Carlos said was only the seventh. Johnny, when drunk, slumped to the left and ran his hands through his hair so that it almost stood on end. Over their seventh or tenth round, they began to tell what I knew were a lot of lies. Johnny said his marriage was blissful and explained Maria's absence by saying that she had the grippe. I was not sure for whose benefit this lie was, since he had told me the week before that they were separated, and it seemed that he and Carlos were friends. It might have been a gratuitous drunken lie, or perhaps Johnny was so chaotic he had forgotten what he had told me. Then Johnny staggered off to the men's room and Carlos told me that he was an orphan who had been adopted in his teens by a pair of Viennese refugees. The only thing he knew about his mother was that she was Mexican—hence Carlos. Then he told me that he had been married twice, first to a singer who was wiped out with their young son in a plane crash, and second to a very sweet, conventional heiress from whom he was divorced. It was too perfect to be true. When Johnny came back, Carlos went to settle up the bill.

"Is all that stuff Carlos told me true?" I said to Johnny.

"If he says it is."

"Well, he's *your* pal. Is it, or isn't it?"

"If he says it is, it is," said Johnny, who was whispering at this point.

I looked around and saw myself in the dim, blue-lit mirror. Here I was drinking with an old pal of my late husband's and a newspaperman. Around the corner were my cheerful friendly digs, my fireplace, my wedding china. I felt as if I had wakened from a dream and found myself in the tropics. When I looked across the table at Johnny Porter, he had on his face the closest thing his mild, repressed prep school features could manufacture in the way of a leer. He looked positively evil and pimpish. For a moment I felt as vulnerable as I had ever felt in my life, alone at a bar with a drunken liar and a lying stranger.

Someone put a dime in the jukebox, and Hank Williams sang "Half as Much." If I had had any sense, I would have left. After all, wasn't I a widow? Didn't I have some urgent mourning to do at home? Didn't I look across the crumpled cigarette packages, sticky glasses, and swizzle sticks at Johnny Porter with a jolt of something closely resembling hatred and suspicion? But I knew I wasn't going to leave. I wanted to sit the evening out, and when Carlos Warren came ambling back, gave me a wide smile of inappropriate affection, and said, "You look like you could use a decent meal in a clean and cheerful place," I realized I was in the grip of a king-sized crush.

XI We had our dinner in a cheap Italian restaurant that was cheerful enough, but neither Carlos nor Johnny was very much interested in food.

"I'd like to be a helluva lot drunker than I am now," Johnny said. "Food brings me down."

"Eat your meal, my son," said Carlos. "You have to eat, if you're going to drink. It's the principle of feeding your nerves. Under the line of fire, it's always wise to have something in your gut. Get him to eat, Olly. Spoonfeed our boy."

We polished off two bottles of wine, and by the time we finished dinner our little group was typecast. Johnny played the sloppy, wayward child who needed attending to. I played the intelligent girl guide who made sure Johnny did not say appalling things to the waitress and who brought a little tone to the group. Carlos played the object of hero worship, with brilliant condescension. It wasn't real life at all.

I felt like a child let out of school, or someone whose past had been rubbed away. I wasn't someone who had ever been married, or who had a personal history. I was only myself in a moment of time, a curly-haired girl wearing a suede skirt, out on the town with a pair of irrelevant drunks, watching, without much interest, the bad boy of our group making himself worse, and observing with a kind of riveted, witless interest that good-looking half-human, Carlos Warren, who could have been filed under Journalists, *see* War Correspondents. If he hadn't been so good at it, he would have been downright arch. He smoked cigars, little twisted cigars from an ornate tin—cigars from Ceylon, which could not, of course, be purchased in the United States. You got them through the diplomatic pouch, or from your pals who flew in from Southeast Asia. He smoked with studied casualness. Under the small table, our knees collided. Johnny slumped back in his chair, shredding a paper napkin.

"You look like the last survivor of an earthquake," said Carlos to Johnny. "I think we ought to get you home."

"I want another drink," said Johnny.

"If you have another drink, my son, you'll turn into a lizard and have to crawl home. Ask for the check, Olly, and let's bail out."

We got Johnny out into the cold. His shirt was open, his tie had disappeared, and he was half in and half out of his coat. When we crossed the street, I realized that we were all drunk, and Johnny was only drunkest. He sulked between us. He didn't want to go home, he wanted another drink, he wanted to sit in the middle of the street and tie his shoes.

"You're a crashing bore, sonny," Carlos said. "Stop making it so difficult for me and this ennobling woman to carry you home. Now, haul ass."

Johnny lived a good walk away, and Carlos figured the fresh air would sober him up. His building was a brick walk-up, and his apartment clearly that of a nice young couple, but it was also clear that one half of the nice couple had up and split. In the bedroom, the closet door was open and only Johnny's suits hung in a neat line, next to a row of empty hangers, some askew. Hung on a peg was a yellow nightgown and on the closet floor was a black evening dress, packed into a lidless box. In the living room there was a stack of old copies of Vogue, tied up to be thrown out. When you got to the kitchen you saw that Maria had taken most of the pots and pans. A skillet and an enamel egg pan were all that was left on a hanging rack.

We dumped Johnny gently on his unmade bed. Above it was a large white square of wall where a painting had been taken down. I left Carlos to deal with Johnny and sat in the living room to wait. It was a hopeful room, that living room, with a grandmother clock, and a painted chest, and some chic, unsittable wicker chairs. Hanging from the ceiling on a wire was a glass wind chime. I looked out the window, and Carlos came up behind me.

"He's down for the count," he said. "Flat out."

He put his arm around me to guide me down the stairs. "What are we going to do now?" he said.

I said, "What do you want to do?"

"Either get drunk or get laid," he said.

"Let's get drunk."

"It's all the same to me," said Carlos. "Let's get a cab and go over to the South Africa."

So I was alone with him—another event. Everything seemed calculated from the time Sam died: my first appearance in public, the first time I had the heart to play the piano, my first time out on the town. In the taxi, he gave me a seductive feline smile, a smile that said: "What a refreshment you are to my jaded sensibilities." What did I think I was doing? I should have stopped the cab and gone home, but I was the former wife of the More Life Kid. I was the More Life Kid. I wanted to hit the South Africa and hang around, getting drunker. I wanted to see what the rest of the evening would bring me. I wanted Carlos Warren to kiss me and I wanted him to follow me up the stairs to my apartment and make me an offer I could not refuse. I wanted him to seduce me, or me him. I wanted some big-time break between me and the world, between the death of Sam and the life of me. Carlos didn't know the difference between me and seven hundred other women in New York. He didn't know that I was a widow, or maybe he did. Maybe Johnny had told him, but enough time and drink had passed between him and that fact, and me. Besides, what did it matter? You aren't what you have passed through, but only what you are, and I was only a girl in a taxi, late at night.

The South Africa was a large, bare, whitewashed bar and the lighting made its patrons look like existentialists. On the window was a little neon sign that said "Shills."

I said, "Why is it called the South Africa if the sign says Shills?"

"It's owned by Gladys Shills," Carlos said. "She's a South African expatriate. A lot of exiles hang out here."

It didn't look like the sort of place that sponsors loud good times. The stark walls bleached the joy and mellowness out of everyone's face. You could sit at the long wooden bar, or you could sit, at a good remove from your fellows, at a number of round wooden tables. These tables were taken up by serious-looking couples and trios, wearing denim and corduroy, and Africans in bluejeans and *batik*. At the end of the bar sat Gladys herself, a large impassive blond woman wearing a leopard coat and a pair of green plush slippers. She nodded at Carlos when we walked in. No one spoke above a whisper, and the jukebox offered quiet, cerebral jazz. It was the most depressing bar I had ever been in. It had the beaten, serious air of a study hall in high school.

Carlos ordered a pair of cognacs and I began to slide a little in my seat. I was less drunk than tired and I felt relatively disarranged, as if my clothes had suddenly stopped fitting. Carlos, of course, was exactly as he had been the moment I met him. No amount of wear or tear or liquor had any effect on him. His natty blazer was still buttoned and had not been unbuttoned all evening. Clean cuffs showed at the end of his sleeves. His tie was still straight. His eyes were more vacant than strained, and when I looked into them, I saw how ruthless they were. When he smiled, he revealed beautiful white teeth.

I drank my cognac and thought about the girls I had gone to school with, the nice ones whose social expectations and emotional lives walked hand in hand in some well-ordered universe, who knew what place they were destined for and sat neatly in it, who were not prone to wayward notions or desires. Girls I had gone to school with were now lawyers and doctors and captains of industry for all I knew, or married to them, but they still smiled benignly above their neat collars. If they had been recently widowed, they would not have found themselves at a morbidly lit bar for expatriate South Africans with an unknown journalist of dubious moral posture for whom they were in the grip of lust. Nor would they feel that they might die if the unknown war correspondent didn't kiss them. They were neat in their neat places and I saw for that instant that Sam was both my places: he kept me placed, but on the side I wanted. It seemed too much to think that danger would ever be so tamely incorporated into my life again.

As we sipped our drinks, Carlos talked about being in the line of fire, or rather, I grilled him. It did not amaze me how deep my interest in this matter went, and it did not surprise me how seductive his well-worked riff was.

"Life is very stripped down," he said. "You know the meaning of gut friendship. It's completely nihilistic. There's no reason for anyone to do anything for anyone else, but they do. It's sheer survival, so if someone hands you a cigarette, you carry that gesture around forever. There are no frills. No niceties. None of the chatter and shadow boxing you have to do in the real world. I've had very intense friendships with guys whose names I never knew."

I said, "How do you get along in the real world after that?"

"It isn't the real world," he said. "That's the real world. Coming back is like coming to another planet. You have to learn to socialize all over again, and you realize how much time you waste getting along with all these flabby fatheads. Contact between two people, or just between people, should be more elementary. Life in the world is just one goddam cocktail party. It's a big fucking waste of time, because we're all under the gun, after all."

He gave me, full force, an expression of bitter sadness, and I smiled back at him. It was better than having a theatrical company playing just for you, but his every word rang in my teenage heart. He wasn't believable at all, but I could have taken a bath in what he said. I was girl darling to boy war correspondent, and as I looked at him I knew that somewhere, probably in some swank modern apartment, he had a wife working herself into a fury over him. He smiled and his beautiful teeth gleamed. No matter how much I knew I was being softened up, that he knew exactly what stops to pull, that he was a real stray in the world, I wanted him. He looked me deeply in the eyes, and I saw again how cold and disinterested his were.

"Let's get out of here," he said.

"I have to go home," I said. It was three o'clock in the morning.

"That's where we're going," he said.

In my apartment, I got the kiss I wanted, and it was pretty gut-crunching, I thought.

"I want you," he said into my ear.

"You'd want anyone who was standing here and female."

He pinned me by my shoulders to the wall and kissed me again.

"We could be very good together," he said, and I silently agreed.

This was the logical conclusion. After a certain age, you don't just get kissed, and after a certain age, things become very stripped down between two people. There was no reason for me to turn him down. It wasn't a question of honor, and this was not, after all, the line of fire. I was torn up with pure lust. There was no morality to cover it, and my only shame was that I was going to say no and chalk myself up squarely with the rest of the ninnies and teases of the world.

"It can't be," I said.

"Why do you say that?" he said. "What's the point of that?" He stroked my hair. "Don't be so silly," he said, at which point I began to cry. I put my arms against him and wept into his blazer. Whatever he thought of this, he held me close and stroked my back.

"I'm sorry," I said. "I didn't mean to cry all over you. I haven't been out much, so I'm a little scrambled."

He looked at me with scorn and disbelief. It was clear that he didn't have the vaguest idea what I meant, and he didn't much care. It was the perfect moment for me to tilt my tear-stained face into the dim light and explain that I had been recently, tragically widowed, that my emotional condition was delicate, and to explain the deep seriousness with which I took passionate connections between women and men, but I hated myself as those convenient words came to me. This was my show, mine alone. Besides, you can't make personal connections with those who don't put any stock by them, and it was my own fault for diving around town with Carlos Warren.

But I didn't have to explain anything to him. He was only a stranger who wanted to shack up late at night. It didn't matter if his desire was general or specific, but I felt obliged to explain nonetheless, and the reason was that he had struck in me real physical longing. I could see that he was puzzled and bored—but mostly bored—and I was in despair. How wantonly I wanted to be understood, and how deeply uninterested he was in whatever I was going to say. He wanted what he wanted at the moment, and what he wanted was not some complicated moral justifying from a young woman he rightly suspected of being a tease.

But my reasons weren't so high-handed after all. It wasn't only the Sams of the world who got their Lyle Crosbys. I had had my Lyle Crosby too, and his name was Richard Cruise.

Richard Cruise was one of the landmarks of my college. He was a lean, wiry man who lived in a stone house in the country and did some casual, gentlemanly farming. He had his friends among the county gentry, the county arts and letters rustics and some of the faculty who had put down local roots. He was sometimes seen driving his beat-up Rover up the college drive when the head of the English department gave dinner parties. He was in his thirties, he was alone, and he had a look of mournful boyishness that gave rise to considerable erotic speculation and fantasy among the more sultry and artistic of my classmates. Occasionally he took a solitary beer in the college bar and you sometimes found him in the afternoon drinking in a dark corner with the writer in residence or the professor of sculpture.

He crossed everyone's mind, and when he crossed mine, I struck a chord of something very like hero worship: the sight of someone so cut off inflamed my most romantic imagination and it seemed to me heroic that he could do without. My room was cluttered with my possessions, my life was cluttered with my friends, but I imagined the life of Richard Cruise to be as sparse and neat as a Japanese brush painting. He came and went as he pleased—for months he wasn't seen at all. He seemed to have invented his own rules of order, and although he smiled at the bar or waved if you passed him on the road, he was as remote as a boulder that weathers time alone.

I met up with him one day by chance at a bar and grill in a town called Plattshook. Plattshook was five miles from campus, and I was taking a serious late autumn walk. By the time I got there, I was ravenous. The bar and grill was a rundown, faded place and Richard Cruise was having a beer at a table by himself when I walked in. He nodded at me, and when I got my hamburger, he motioned for me to come and sit with him since we were the only people around. We spent the afternoon feeding dimes to Conway Twitty on the jukebox and talking about college. This was around the time that I was getting sick of Eddie Liebereu, when life looked a little too assured and shapely for my comfort. I had the fine, gray day to myself, and Richard Cruise was its private treasure.

He told me that he had spent his childhood summers in the area, and after college, after graduate school, and after six months in the Marines and a year working in Boston, he had decided to come back. We talked about my professors. By the time we finished our extended chat, it was dusk and he offered to drive me back to school.

We took the scenic route by the river, and when we passed his house, which you could just see the roof of from the road, he asked if I would like to come in, and I said yes. It was a stone house with small rooms and in the living room was a gray marble fireplace on which a garland of flowers had been carved. We sat in his spare kitchen drinking coffee, and when it got dark we made omelettes on the wood stove. It was not at all odd to be there, but nothing was said about it except that he asked if he was keeping me from anything at school and I said no. I was afraid that if I questioned my own presence in his house, the bubble would be broken and I would find myself teleported to my college room. I showed him how to flip an omelette, and he told me he made his own catsup and applesauce. He was not even marginally seductive. It was simply a break in ordinary life for both of us, and he was boyish enough to be the sort of polite, shy friend your brother brings home at mid-semester break. But his house seeped into me: it was bare and broody and smelled of ash. His worn tweed jacket smelled of woodsmoke.

He was cut off all right, but he was very polite and we kept up a breezy, flowing conversation that made me feel terrifically uncomfortable, since you never got to the heart of anything with him, and at that stage of my life, connection was all. There was nothing in his manner that made me understand why he wanted me around, but he didn't make any gesture to get me back to school. He announced his ways, his rules of order, and his priorities with such bearing and silence that it seemed to me intrusive not to float along with them, so I floated.

After dinner, he showed me the artifacts he had bought with the house: the hooked rugs, the whale oil lamp, the wooden closet doors that had boating scenes painted on them, and a trio of stuffed birds perched on a branch under a large glass bell.

We sat in front of the fire and drank brandy, and when we stopped to see what time it was, we were amazed to find that it was after curfew, so it was arranged, out of necessity, that I spend the night. I spent it in his bed—there was no other bed and the couch was too hard and small to sleep on—and began it by wearing one of his soft, faded work shirts. It is hard to get comfortable next to a stranger, even if you have sat with him for hours, especially if in those hours you never cross the bridge from politeness into friendship. Sometime during that night we turned to each other and his work shirt fell to the floor, and for all that we had not crossed the bridge into friendship, we crossed some other bridge into the kind of passion that does not need intimacy in order to thrive. When we woke, the sky was solid gray and we faced each other with the same intensity.

By noon we were dressed, and Richard Cruise asked me what I liked for breakfast, if I liked my toast light or dark and what I took in my coffee. We had toast and jam, over which we discussed the misery of my college's soccer team and its humiliation by a bunch of seminarians from St. Joseph's of the Cross. That sexual fire didn't tear down any walls. It only made us more formal. I told him I would walk back to school but he drove me to the top of the college road, since he had errands to do, and gave me a painless kiss on my cheek.

From time to time, I saw him at the bar and we always smiled. For a couple of months during the winter he was not around, but one spring day we sat and had a drink together. He asked me how my classes were going. It was all stiff and friendly, but that one-night stand confused my notion of things. How could we have been so passionate if we had still been strangers, and how could we still be strangers with all that passion between us? The event had its place for him—it ended where it ended. The only thing we had in common was the landscape and a mutual admiration for the vocal works of Conway Twitty. Even though I had spent a night in his bed, I had no idea if he had committed the act between us to his mind or heart. It shook me to my bones; it seemed so random, so extraordinary, and so able to be shelved. Carlos Warren brought it all back.

Finally I didn't care what I said, so I told Carlos Warren that I had been recently widowed, and after looking at me with what appeared to be real sympathy, he clutched me again. It didn't matter what you said to him—no truth or lie got in his way. He didn't have much in the way of emotion to affect, so what could you appeal to? Besides, his stance was reasonable enough. Wasn't it late at night? Wasn't this the apartment of an unattached woman? Hadn't we been hanging out all evening?

"You're a real weird kid," he said.

"This is my first night out on the town. I'm sorry."

"Don't be sorry," he said. "You're a very nice person." And on that note of chilling cordiality, he left.

When he was gone, I stalked my apartment in the grip of something that made me want to trash the place. I wanted to break up the furniture, stomp on the china, and watch the glasses as they shattered brilliantly against the fireplace. It wasn't just desire or denial.

When in my room at college I brooded about Richard Cruise, I had felt bereft and unworthy. He was the solitary other and I had had the chance to puncture his solitude, but I had failed. When I met Sam, he was available; he had the same remoteness, and I had won. They were excessive types, and so was Carlos Warren. To get through to them, to connect with them seemed to me a feat that singled you out and branded you with specialness. A gesture from them was the decoration you got after an act of courage.

You cannot be a secret champion of excess without being excessive yourself, and the state I had worked myself into over Richard Cruise returned to me in memory as I paced the room, looking for something fragile enough to throw against the wall.

It was only Sam's conventional, evasive side that saved me, that got me him. Now he was where he belonged, as lost as Richard Cruise, as ungettable, as unobtainable. Carlos Warren was one more excessive, inaccessible stranger who liked to live on any suitable knife-edge, cut off in a stone house, on a bored-out Vincent Black Shadow, or directly in the line of fire. I was there too, not on the sidelines, but in the midst of them, grinning the smile of an innocent appreciator, my hot excessive heart flashing admiration. That's where I belonged, and that's where I had put myself, like those injured jaywalkers who tell you they were drawn into the traffic.

XII On the weekends I worked over my notes for Max Price, practiced the piano, and cruised the neighborhood for domestic items I didn't need. I bought an unnecessary French teakettle and an overpriced basket from Zaire. Nothing sold in Greenwich Village seemed to be American in origin, but at the end of Bleecker Street was a good old U.S.A. general store that sold bluejeans, work jackets, and underwear. There I found a pair of men's pajamas so lovable I almost bought them. They had red stripes, and between the stripes a vertical rank of giraffes wearing crash helmets. I stood at the counter contemplating them until I realized the depths of my self-indulgence and left.

Every few weeks I got on the train and went to visit my parents. These visits were agreeable enough: my parents struggled valiantly against normal worry, and I struggled valiantly against the threat of loving invasion. But they only said that I looked thin and so provided large cheering meals, or said that I looked pensive and so engaged me in games of backgammon or midnight gin rummy. To lift my spirits, my mother took me shopping, my father read grim items from the newspaper in the voice of Groucho Marx, and we took bracing walks in the afternoon. But they didn't press to find out what I was up to, and since I was not in danger, they were calmed to see me recovering slowly.

I spent some time reflecting, with real despair, on Carlos Warren, that typecast flash in the pan. I knew I would never see him again, unless I happened to bump into him during a revolution in the Sudan, but my encounter with him gave me what my father called "cause for pause."

Just as I had been Sam's wedge, the door of evasion he closed between himself and the world, so he was mine. Left to my own devices, what would I have done? Run around cracking my heart against the grim, engaging smiles of heartless punks like Carlos Warren is what I would have done. Sam kept me steady: he kept me from giving my impulses a good run for their money since he came so close to what I craved. I loved outlaws or anybody who looked like one. I liked anything with a hard edge on it. I'd take a cowboy if there weren't any Indians around, but Indians were smarter, angrier, had better horses, and didn't need a saddle when they rode. Confronted with the nice tame faces at Butler Library or at a concert hall, a yearning for mayhem welled in me, and I knew it was better to be excessive. It was better to fall into harm's arm than to snuggle up with safety and mildness. But Sam hadn't been very wild, actually. He wasn't very dangerous at all; Carlos Warren was the hard core. Sam's dealings with danger were all flirtation, while Carlos conducted the serious love affair. He had been shot at, strafed, bombed nearby. He had been thrown out of several banana republics and jailed in Rhodesia. His nerves, if he had any, were made of catgut, not steel; his wildness was dead set, and he was heartless as a result. But I had never outgrown the belief that life is best performed by gemlike flames, and Sam was a domestic variety.

Carlos Warren made me realize how valuable Sam was, and the useless love and longing for him that burned inside me almost did me in. I thought I had missed him, but I hadn't known what missing was. In a world of Carlos Warrens, I wanted Sam, and I spent three weeks in desolation as solid as a stone fence. I was relapsing heavily.

At which point Patrick turned up. He had been away on business and was friskier than I had ever seen him. He appeared one Sunday afternoon, armed with his Nikon camera and several rolls of film. I told him that I was not up for any outdoor photographic expedition, but he said it was a brand-new camera and he had brought it over to try it out on me. I was low and worn out—wounded—and did not feel like a proper subject for a new camera, but Patrick bullied me into a chair and arranged me. He adjusted the shutters and switched the lights on and off. I didn't want my picture taken. I wanted to be carted into the street and shot like a dog, but Patrick didn't care. When he got bored with a sitting subject, he allowed me to move around and followed me. Nothing was about to get in the way of his buoyant spirits. I had never seen him like this, and I wondered what was the cause of it, but Patrick never explained why or what he felt. He only broadcast it.

I didn't know anything about Patrick. The tie between us didn't make us close; it only held us close. I didn't have to get to know Patrick; I already knew him. But when I contemplated the sum total of my knowledge, I came up empty. Across the room, he was unloading his camera, as private as a bank vault, possessor of a rich history I knew nothing about.

I said, "Where have you been keeping yourself, Patrick?"

"I've been working," he said. "I had to go to Washington a couple of times. There's nothing like complicated litigation to keep your brain poised and wreck your body. What have you been up to?"

"Nothing much. I've been working for Max and going up to the library."

"And you've been alone except for that?"

"I've been out a little."

"That's good to hear," he said brightly. "Who with?"

I told him I had been out with an old college pal of Sam's and he pressed me for a name. When I told him Johnny Porter, he said, "That jerk."

Then he asked after my parents.

"Are they giving you any trouble?" he said.

"What's that supposed to mean?"

"It means are they asking you what your plans are."

"What is this? Some kind of third degree?"

Patrick said, "It's getting hard to have a normal conversation with you, Elizabeth."

"I'm sick and tired of being the center of everyone's concern."

"We like to see our Elizabeth making life-affirming gestures," Patrick said. "We don't like her to be cloaked away from life."

"Last week I went to bed with a war correspondent," I said. "Is that life-affirming enough for you?"

"Did you?" asked Patrick in a tone of total condescension. When I didn't answer, he asked again.

"None of your fucking business," I said.

"Really, Elizabeth. It would be a good thing for you to mess around a little more."

"I can't see why we're having this conversation, Patrick. I didn't go messing around with anyone, for your information, but I can't stand this constant picking over me."

He put his arm around me. "A little hostility is better than nothing at all. When I came in, you looked like the last day. I only goaded you a little, to get you going. Now, if you would give some thought to getting out of your jeans and into some respectable clothes, I'd take you out for a very lush meal."

He grinned sweetly, and I felt a pang of pure rage.

"I'm not some psychological experiment. I won't be power played. Goddammit, Patrick, what do you think I am?"

He endured this, still grinning. A couple of weeks between us and he had lost both his casualness and his stiffness. Patrick, when he wasn't being formal or offhand, was simply comfortable, and in any of those states he wasn't approachable. He was as opaque and standoffish as vitreous china.

He said, "I hate to see you looking so closed off. I only wanted to stir you up. I figured you must have been through some recent bad times. Go get dressed and I'll apologize over dinner."

At a quiet restaurant with plush banquettes, we finished off a bottle of burgundy. Throughout the meal, Patrick was at me:

he led the conversation like a dancing master, and by the time we got to coffee, we were earnestly on the subject of Max Price's book. Not one personal word was said. We didn't talk about Sam or family or ourselves. We talked about work, and Patrick smiled his smug and impish smiles. He wasn't like Patrick at all, although he was enormously pleased with himself. After dinner, he saw me home and it was the first time since Sam died that I did not get ritually kissed goodnight. He said, "One of my colleagues has a darkroom, so I'll call you next week after I develop the pictures and I wouldn't turn down an invitation for dinner." Then he was gone.

What I felt when he left was a mixture of anger, gratitude, and puzzlement. Patrick got the jump on you, I thought, which wasn't fair, but on the other hand, he had gotten me out of an awful state of despair. My dinner with him had been actively enjoyable. He had made me angry enough to shout. He had taken me out into the world, at least for the evening, that devious and secret operator.

A week later he called to say that the photographs were ready and that he would very much like to have roast chicken and steamed escarole, if I didn't mind, and I didn't.

If I had thought about it, I would have expected the photos in a manila envelope, but Patrick brought them in a black cardboard folio tied with black cotton ribbon.

"I know you don't like to be the center of everyone's concern, but there you are," said Patrick.

I opened the folio under the light, and when I looked at the prints, there was something about them I could not define. They ran from the mawkish to the hostile to the sorrowful to a big, open smile, and some of them had no expression at all. It seemed to be a record of everything I was capable of, and it shocked me. They were black and white photos, but the light in them looked sweet, like that honey-colored light you see on white marble in museums with skylights. When I looked through them again, I could not recognize the self I saw, the self I knew or thought I knew. In anthropology you learn that some primitive tribes think the camera takes your soul away, and I could see why. I felt that my soul had been not only taken away, but also given back to me.

"They're beautiful, aren't they?" Patrick said. "My best work." All I could do was nod. Then he closed the cover, tied the ribbons, and asked for his dinner.

He still had his high spirits. In fact, he was positively jaunty, but he was restless too. Over coffee, he told me that Sara had gone to Paris.

I said, "For a vacation?"

"For a year," he said. "Maybe two." I felt as if an anvil had been thrown at me.

"She told me to tell you she was sorry not to have called, but she was in Boston and then in Chicago, and then she had to do a crash translation." He poured himself another cup of coffee and the light gleamed off his gold cufflinks.

"Don't you care?"

"She's always wanted to live in Paris," Patrick said.

"I thought you two were fixed."

"We were fixed to unfix, when we wanted to."

"I thought you were going to get married one of these days."

"Sara and I wouldn't ever have married," Patrick said.

"Then why did you hang around so long?"

"We weren't made for permanence," Patrick said. "We got along very well, but for all the wrong reasons. We appealed to each other's sense of finiteness, and we both knew it. She's been planning to go to Paris for a year or so."

This was not information I wanted to have. It disturbed my sense of things. Sara and Patrick were as permanent as a landmark building, and the fact that they could no longer be considered coupled scared me.

Patrick made a fire and I did the dishes, discovering in the process that my hands were shaking slightly, but I didn't know why. My father, when I was young, once described me to a woman who doted on me as the most self-conscious child he had ever known, and I still was. Deep in my heart, I knew I had the goods on me. I knew what I was all about but why was

I standing in a kitchen feeling shaky? I had kept Patrick pegged in my mind as unapproachable and private, and when he was around, I made sure he stayed that way. Now he had hit me with a piece of hard information and I was in danger of smashing one of the nice crystal wine glasses some well-heeled crony of my parents had forked over as a wedding present.

Patrick pulled up two armchairs in front of the fire and put a hassock between them to rest our feet on. We drank our coffee and Patrick cut apple slices and threw the peels into the fire. It was my turn to do some asking, but I balked. I didn't want to know what went on between him and Sara, so we sat quietly until Patrick asked if he could put on some music. We listened to Boccherini with our feet up. Patrick sat there quietly, not smiling, but smoothed out. The room smelled of woodsmoke and apple. The light from the fire played over his face. His hair fell onto his forehead and he looked not sleepy, but contemplative.

"If everyone sat in front of a fire once a week," he said, "the people who make tranquillizers would go out of business."

I said, "You can always come over here and have a fire, if you want."

"That's very polite of you, and I may take you up on it, now that the crunch is over at work."

"That's fine with me," I said.

"I'm quite sure it's not fine," said Patrick. "You don't want someone running in and out of your home lighting fires. I'll wait for a formal invitation."

"You don't need a formal invitation."

"Yes I do," said Patrick. "Now give me my photos. It's time to go home."

"I thought those were for me."

"Of you," said Patrick. "Not for you. Those are mine."

The next day I sat at my table in the stacks reading under the desk lamp. My pile of three-by-five cards was growing daily, and I had gone through several legal pads. But I wasn't thinking about chamber music in America. I was thinking about Patrick or, rather, trying not to. Something had changed between us, or within him, and I didn't know what it was or what difference it made. I took Patrick seriously, and it affected me. Patrick, after all, was the deep one, according to family myth, the deep and private one. I knew his good opinion meant a lot to me. I knew I had it, but I didn't know why. He made me shy, but the most self-conscious child my father had ever seen, the More Life Widow of the More Life Kid, was more than shy. She was panicked.

When the rug is swept out from under you, you hang for an instant between standing and falling, and for that instant, there is nothing solid or dependable in the world: if you lose your balance, you lose everything. Sitting there making my notes, listening to the shuffle of books being arranged on the carts, to two library workers having a whispered fight about the basketball game, it occurred to me that thinking about Patrick without Sara upset me considerably, and it did not satisfy anything to think that my reaction was only to a rearrangement in the normal order. But if that wasn't the reason, what was? I had no answer to give myself, so I went back to my research, with the shaky feeling you have when you get out of a small plane after several hours in the air.

XIII Henry Jacobs and Max Price had been friends all their lives. They had grown up together in Chicago, had gone to college together, and when they traveled they sent each other what they called "loony postcards." These postcards contained either cryptic messages or dopey greetings and had pictures of golden porcupines or Dungeness crabs or cows wearing bonnets or natives having a lobster race or can-can girls from the Follies. If you knew Max or Henry well enough, they would drag out their postcards for you, if things got dull.

When Henry came to New York, Max invited me for dinner. His wife was in New Haven for a Russian seminar, so we were left at the mercy of the Prices' housekeeper, Fritzie Bettes, a middle-aged woman from Kentucky, who felt, Max told me, that she was the only competent person alive and that, without her, the Prices, her husband, and countless others would decline on the spot. If she baked a pie at home, she put another in the oven for the incompetent Prices. Since Max was having company for dinner and Mrs. Price was out of town, Fritzie Bettes had left a roast in the oven, potatoes and string beans on the stove, and one of her pies as well as precise printed instructions on when to put the light under what and how to properly serve. As I came in, she was leaving. She wore an old wool turban and had a cigarette smoldering at the corner of her mouth.

"Goodbye, Max," she said. "See that you do everything according to the book."

Max introduced us. "These men," she said to me, and left.

Max took me into the living room, where Henry was having a drink and watching the evening news. He stood to kiss me and said, "How's Patrick?"

"Very charged up," I said.

"He's a terrific find," Henry said. "The law professor's dream." Henry couldn't talk about either Sam or Patrick without making a brief speech, and his statement of the evening was that Sam was lovable, but Patrick commanded love. The effect of this on me was a great desire to have the subject changed. My feelings about Patrick included hostility, fear, and suspicion in equal measure. He took me to the movies. He made me play all the themes and variations in a Mozart rondo that had taken his fancy. He teased and provoked and insulted, and darted around like a gnat, caught up in his own good mood. I put up with this because I owed it to him, because I was lonely, and because I was waiting for my sudden evil feelings to fly away and leave me and Patrick level again. But his good spirits ran very close to smugness, I felt, and his casual revelation about Sara's departure ran close to the sinister. Furthermore, his provocations were effective. He got a solid reaction out of me, and while he pulled me out of true despair, all he left me with was fright. When I stopped to think about it, which was as infrequently as my relentless mind would allow, I realized that my reactions didn't make much sense. He was only my brother-in-law, my quasi-pal, who led a life of his own and was kind enough to want to tease a sorrow-stricken sister-in-law out of melancholy.

But the subject was changed. The evening news was over and the three of us went into the kitchen to see what wonders Fritzie Bettes had wrought.

"After Fritzie's been here, it doesn't seem to be our kitchen any more," Max said. "We're waging a proprietary war with her. We put things away, and she comes and puts them where *she* thinks they ought to be. When we finally find what we need, we put it back and wait for her to undo it. It's all very affable, though. See if you can find a large white platter. It was on the top of the icebox, but God only knows where she's put it."

Finally, we sat to dinner, and Max and Henry launched into a brisk conversation about wine prices. After that we got down to serious eating, and during a lull in the conversation Max said, "Now, Olly. I didn't invite you here just to see Henry. We have some business to discuss."

"What business?"

"Well, you've done wonderful work for me and I think it's time you got out of the library and into the musical world a little."

"I'm only an amateur," I said.

"That doesn't matter," Max said. "You're a serious person and there's a lot you could do. Now Henry and I have been discussing this behind your back and here's what we thought. There's a musical foundation that sponsors the Hamilton Conservatory—one of the smaller ones. It's in New Hampshire, and they meet at the end of the summer. It's by invitation or recommendation only, so it's quite an elite group. Henry and I would like to recommend you. Besides, they have a wonderful small library and you could do some work for me. What do you say?"

I didn't say anything. There I sat between two kindly men in their sixties who were arranging life for my betterment. I said I'd think it over and thanked them. Then Max mentioned that Patrick was stopping by for coffee, and a black curtain of adolescent fury came flapping over my eyes. Suddenly, Max and Henry were not kindly mentors but strangers, blind to what was brewing inside me as I sat politely at their table. In that company, I was only a nice-looking girl, doing competent research, not some roiling teen queen working up to some piercing hostility. Why was Patrick coming for coffee? It seemed to me that was all he ever did. He showed up, like some awful dog who took a liking to you and stuck to your side. I was going to be plagued all my days by Patrick appearing after dinner. If I moved to Tashkent and lived in a yurt, Patrick would appear out of the desert for Turkish coffee. And Max and Henry would stop by to see if I had made any musicological notes on the flute patterns of the local tribesmen. I was deeply angry and ashamed.

But when Patrick appeared, for about three minutes I wasn't angry at all. The thought of him and his being were two different things. He was courtly and charming, and when I looked at him from my end of the table I realized how wonderful he was to look at.

What was boyish in Sam's face missed being boyish in Patrick's. His eyes were not the wide, hell-bent eyes of someone let out of prep school for the afternoon. He wasn't at all cherubic, as Sam had been. In profile, he looked noble, but rough, and his cheekbones weren't flat like Sam's, but arched. His hair was wavier than Sam's, and his face was so mobile you could have known the story of a movie by watching Patrick watch it. When he smiled—which wasn't often, although he grinned—he was another man. It was a smile with a lot of resonance.

I hated him. I hated his smugness. I hated the way he kept himself a secret and sprang things on you. I hated the fact that he told you his conclusions but not how he came to them. I hated the air he had of having an underground, covert life plan that made perfect and elegant sense to him and *might* be revealed when his perfect sense of time told him he was right to speak. I hated being seen through or having anyone think they could see through me. I hated being under his scrutiny. For all his beautiful smile, what I wanted was not to be understood, but to be left alone—by Patrick specifically. It would have filled me with pleasure to aim a solid right cross at his lovely chin and watch him reel backward in his chair.

But I was a civilized girl in a civilized household. We drank our coffee, sipped our brandy, and talked about the government. When it was time to go, the men shook hands, and I kissed my aged mentors.

Out on the street, Patrick hailed a taxi.

"I can get my own cab," I said.

"It might be *my* cab I'm flagging."

"I'm taking the subway. See you."

Patrick said, "Are you sure you want to take a subway yourself at this hour of the night?"

I turned on him, truly gripped by rage.

"Goddammit, Patrick. I'm sick of having you and everyone else treat me like a cripple. I'm sick of having everything arranged. Why can't you just leave me alone?" A big checker cab stopped at a light and I ran for it, leaving Patrick standing alone on the corner, briefcase in hand.

When I got home, I found in my mailbox an envelope containing a duplicate set of Patrick's photographs of me. I perused them to see if I could find some fault and add a little fuel to my anger. But there weren't any faults. They had been taken with an eye of serious affection, which, in my hateful state, made me feel set upon and condescended to.

Venting rage gives a nice temporary glow, but the aftermath is bitter. I could have consoled myself by thinking that Patrick had no feelings to hurt, but it wasn't so. He was filled with propriety and caution, but that only looks like coldness at a long, long distance. One of life's terrors is to be under the thumb of something incomprehensible, and I was. I had been rude to my brother-in-law, who was all kindness. I imagined him standing on the corner watching me fling my rageful self into the taxi and drive off. I imagined that he was thinking how lucky his family was to have had its connection with me broken; that I was an ungrateful, hysterical girl.

The worst part of emotional life is speculative: I had no information. I was very angry, between puzzlement and fear, inching toward fear. The language between me and Patrick was like a double-edged code. I had counted on his subtlety, on his standoffishness when it suited me. One of the blessings of Sam had been his straightforwardness. I counted on Patrick to be complicated, to work his complications out in private so that I could savor the results—but not up close. I had spent my life watching over my emotional states and everyone else's as if they were emerging Art, and at the bottom of my soul I thought there was no more interesting thing in the world. How I loved and appreciated! At my final hour, the devil, or St. Peter, or some judgmentalist the Jews have planted in heaven would present me with tape recordings of my exegesis and rhapsodies on human conduct, a large portion of which would be devoted to the deeper workings of Sam, the intricacies of Patrick Bax's nature, and of course myself, the lovely widow. I was a timepiece all right. I had the mechanism of one of those tinny watches that breaks down all the time. Patrick would be justified in preparing a brief to state that I was one of the quirkiest and most unpleasant people alive. On that note of Olympian self-hatred, I went to bed and spent half the night half awake and, when asleep, dreaming that I was lost in the stacks at Butler Library.

The next morning, I got as far as dialing Patrick's number and hanging up before it rang. I drank my coffee, assembled my notes, and called his law firm; but when it answered, I hung up again. Then I dragged up to Columbia, feeling alternately cheerful and decayed. After a couple of hours at work, I went to get some air and lunch, and on the way back, I passed a flower shop. It occurred to me that Patrick was not the only master of the open-ended gesture, so I sent to his office a huge, lavish bunch of tea roses and freesias, without a note, only my name scribbled on a pasteboard card. This kept me cheered as I walked back to the library, where I amused myself by browsing through back issues of *Vogue* and reading the *Sonnets to Orpheus*.

My bouquet set me back thirty dollars and allowed me to believe that I had turned my panic into a nice cat and mouse game. Patrick would call. I would be snappish. We would have dinner. And then what? I didn't think past it. If I had had any sense, I would have focused on my brother-in-law only as brother-in-law, but I did not think much about the recipient, who seemed to have conveniently slipped out of classification. But he didn't call.

He didn't call for two weeks, but I went right on grinning until it occurred to me that the flowers might never have been delivered, at which point I called the shop to check. They had been delivered and signed for. This threw a little wrench of panic in the direction of my heart, but introspection had abandoned me, along with my delicate notions of appropriateness. For about five minutes I pondered the excess of my gesture and my extreme reaction to Patrick, but, then, a mood of high-spirited cretinism moved in, and I didn't think at all.

I was as wound up as a toy train until my manic cheerfulness was displaced by a mood of gothic desolation. I began to fear I had alienated Patrick, and that brought me to grief again. I was an immature little flame fanner who would rather have drama than friendship. I was the ninny who would whip up any situation rather than leave it be. The only real thing that had ever happened to me was the death of Sam, and the only unadorned emotion I had ever felt was well and correctly placed grief. But for that, I was a wayward, flighty, dopey kid. When another week went by, I added pride to my list of sins.

I trudged up to the library and dragged home. I ate my meals in silence, practiced the piano, and went over my notes for Max Price. I sat at the piano and composed a little cubist music. I was filled with overblown, implacable emotion.

When I felt I had calmed down, I decided that it was time to apologize to Patrick in person. It had been a month since I'd seen him. In my becalmed state I trusted to instinct, which decided on a rather harebrained plan. On a rainy Saturday toward the end of March, with a sky so dark the streetlights were on, I got on a bus to go puncture Patrick's solitude and deliver myself of some sloppy, guilty sentiments. In all the time I had been in New York, I had never been in Patrick's apartment; he had always come to mine. He lived in a brick house, on the top floor, but as I confronted his building, my courage failed. My convenient fantasies of this event had led me to expect a handy telephone booth on his corner. There was none, and I was far too cowardly to simply ring his bell. Around the corner was a bar I walked slowly to, getting myself good and soaked. There was a nice pay phone in a nice oak booth, in which I sat staring stupidly at the dial. Maybe he wasn't alone. Maybe he was in bed with Sara, suddenly returned from Paris, or someone like her. Maybe he was out, or in but not answering, or had seen me from his window and bolted the door. And if he answered when I called, how was I to know if he would speak to me? Or if he spoke to me, would he tell me roundly to fuck off? I took a deep breath and dialed. It would have served me right if he had been out, but he was in.

He asked me where I was calling from, since there was a lot of clatter in the background, and when I said I was in the bar around the corner from him he said, "You better come up, then." I reflected, on my short walk, that Patrick was not so private as to keep me off his premises. I had expected him to meet me at the bar.

I rang his doorbell and climbed three carpeted flights of stairs. He met me at the top and I stood in the doorway with my coat and umbrella dripping, wearing a battered straw hat I kept for rainy days, looking like the world's wettest fool.

I said, "I came to apologize."

"You're dripping all over the floor," Patrick said.

"I don't want to come in until I've said I'm sorry."

"I'm sorry, too," said Patrick. "I was a little done in by your floral tribute and I've been thinking that I've been awfully condescending to you without meaning to be. I gave you a rough time purposely, but I forget what a private person you are."

"You're very private, too," I said.

"We hermits have to stick together," said Patrick. "Give me your coat."

XIV His apartment was spare and comfortable. He had been working at his desk, which was piled with papers. A lump of cannel coal was burning in the fireplace and on the mantelpiece I was amazed to see a framed picture of me.

"You look like you need a drink," he said, and disappeared into the tiny kitchen. It was disconcerting to be in his exclusive corner of the world, so I looked around at his neat rows of books, the blue Chinese urn—clearly a bequest from his grandmother—and a pottery snail from one of Meridia's craft projects on the other side of the mantel. On one wall he had a watercolor of a house almost hidden by two trees. The trees framed the house in the shape of a Valentine, and if you looked closely, you could see a tiny face at the attic window.

He came back with a bottle of bourbon and two glasses full of ice. We sat in front of the fireplace and drank in silence.

There are things that you know in your blood or in your cells and when they happen they make perfect sense, but the perfectness of that sense makes you reel. We sipped our drinks, and after a long time, I turned to Patrick. He looked like a boy who has read something disturbing and puzzling in a book, or as if he had been musing seriously over a calculus problem and was on the verge of solving it. I think I must have leaned forward in my chair and I think he must have leaned too, for suddenly he took me by the wrist and we were standing with our arms entwined. I felt such a jolt of longing for him that I seemed to lose my bearings. Any connection between us of family or legality or friendship was null and

117

tepid in the face of it. It explained our connection all along; it explained my recent terrors; it explained the odd, shy, but intense bond I had always felt for him.

Then we walked down a small hallway to his bedroom. The roof slanted and the windows were low, blocked by tree branches. You could hear the constant drum of rain on the roof.

I seemed to be only skin. If I had thought about it, I might have realized that there are connections deep enough to terrify. But I didn't think. If there was such a thing as pure feeling, this was it.

He wasn't like Sam. He was only Patrick. Living with Sam, with Sam's death, with grief, had changed me, and until I was with Patrick I didn't know how changed I was. Pleasure requires high and loving spirits and energy, but living in the world—being battered by it—having your heart pierced, sharpens everything. I had grown up without knowing it, and now I knew. I knew that you might believe in rapture, but you had to earn the right to feel it. You had to pay for it with grief and loss, and it was worth it. I knew what it was like to be ultimately close to your best friend on earth, to someone you had waited to know, had watched and calculated, someone well loved and intelligible to you. I had bounced into bed with Sam. Our love had been larks, the loving of two relatively happy and game kids. But this was different. Patrick and I were not children. We were thoughtful adults with a lot on the line, with complicated histories and a long, complicated mutual bond. Being with him was ravishing. It was relief, and it was terrifying.

He smiled a smile so profound it hit me physically, I was so sensitized I realized what the notion dying of joy is all about. It was a smile of total complicity.

We were together for a long time and then Patrick took me gently by my shoulders and said my name, and then I pressed my head against his chest and began to laugh. It was laughter that seemed to start somewhere in the vicinity of my toes and I couldn't stop it: it was the only way my flesh knew to affirm its feelings.

118

We stayed locked together without speaking, and I wondered, when thought returned to us, as normal breathing returns to a runner, what we were going to say. We didn't say anything.

The rain beat down on the roof and against the windows. You could hear the clock ticking softly on the bureau. The room was filled with dark-green light and there was a wet breeze from the corner window. Patrick gleamed in the darkness. He looked beautiful to me, in the way a stranger's beauty takes you by surprise and in the way a well-known face can bring you up short. I wanted that afternoon to suspend itself infinitely, but it was a countdown until reality intervened, even though the weather was on our side. It had been so dark all day you couldn't tell what time it was. The smiles on our faces were of pure triumph, amazement, and delight, but the only recognizable thing that functioned between us was longing, and when we finally unlocked, it was past dinnertime and we were starving.

Patrick captured all the pillows and propped up his head. His smug smile was back in full force; he was himself again.

"I'd like scrambled eggs and bacon and toast and a salad and a bottle of wine and coffee," he said. "Here's the deal. You make dinner. I clean up. For dessert I'd like a chocolate fudge sundae with two scoops of coffee ice cream, and an apple."

"I'll send out for it," I said.

"That's not the plan. The plan is, I go out into the pouring rain to the delicatessen and get ice cream and some of that crummy fudge sauce I'm sure you don't approve of, and when I come back you shower me with kisses and tell me how wonderful I was to go out in the rain and how much you missed me."

I said, "Will you miss me while you're out in the rain, you smug bastard?"

He turned on his side and wrapped his arms around me.

"I love you," he said. "I always have."

We had our dinner and killed a bottle of wine. At the end of dinner, a little clarity had set in and I didn't know what to do.

Patrick refused to let me help clean up, and suddenly I was uncomfortable among his things. I sat in a chair by the window and lit a cigarette, watching the smoke trail to the window and under it and out into the night. When he finished with the dishes, Patrick appeared in front of me holding his raincoat and mine. For an awful moment I thought he was dismissing me.

"Come on," he said. "Let's go get the Sunday paper." I bowed my head while he helped me on with my coat, close to tears of relief. I felt like a child in a Grimm fairy tale approaching the enchanted forest in a spirit of fear and high adventure, left without compass points or a sense of proportion. This wasn't the beginning of an ordinary love affair: I was lost, without props. We walked out into the rain, huddled under Patrick's umbrella. When we disengaged and I watched him buy the Sunday *Times*, I felt there was no more complicity: I was in my own corner. For that ten-minute walk, I didn't know how to behave, but Patrick was effortless, unruffled, and happy. When he took my arm, I wondered if he was about to put me in a taxi and send me home. But we walked back, he unfurled his umbrella, dumped the papers into my arms, and kissed me. We walked up the stairs to his apartment with our arms locked. He whistled. I brooded.

By rights, I should have been as comfortable as a cat. I was a cherished presence, in the company of someone who loved me. I spent Sunday curled up on the sofa and read the sports section while Patrick read The News of the Week in Review. It rained all day and we stretched out like two big cats in the sun, barely speaking, perfectly attuned. After a good, long dinner, we drank some brandy and went to bed.

There is terror and there is joy and there is something that can be either; it takes you out of your own skin. If I had had to find a word for it, I would have known that it was ecstasy. It was nothing you could summon up: it happened to you and you were in its grip. I was old enough to know what my emotional range was, and I was used to it. Even grief was something I had incorporated and tamed: it and love and hate and anger and tenderness and fear and happiness had been domesticated, I had lived with them so long. But I could never have conjured this: it took me by storm, by flash flood. It seemed to me that I had been cohabiting silently with some very intense impulse toward Patrick, so deep I hadn't known where it slumbered, and it frightened me. It was awesome to think that I had contained something this rich and not known it. It seemed to me that this was the sum total of everything I had ever thought about him, or depended upon him for, or brooded over or admired. It explained my terror when he had told me Sara was going away. Falling asleep, I thought I had been through an epiphany, and that event had opened up the world to joy and chaos.

When I woke, I felt translucent. Patrick woke me up with a cup of coffee. I had slept through his alarm.

"Get serious," he said. "It's Monday. How are we going to arrange ourselves this week?"

"Am I being presented with another plan?" I was half awake and only meant to tease, but I must have struck some nerve.

"What I mean is, we ought to see how much time we want to spend together." He said it so softly I had to put my head on his shoulder to hear him. "I just thought if we made some arrangement, we wouldn't have to go through the awkwardness of making arrangements."

This struck a nerve in me. How ardently I assumed he had the upper hand, and now he sat beside me, ardently assuming that I had. But neither of us had any hand at all: we were both slightly panicked. It made him more level in my eyes, and I realized that we were on equal ground. So before I cranked up my mental faculties, I wanted to lie back and loll in the ease of it. I sipped my coffee, balancing the saucer on my knees. Patrick was wearing a half-buttoned shirt and the trousers to his sober lawyer's suit. I put my cup on the floor and fixed him with an intent look. I realized I had several seconds of pure tease to enjoy, so I simply smiled and didn't speak. Then I locked my arms around his neck.

"I don't even want you to go to work," I said. "I want you to call up and say that you have a debilitating disease and have to stay in bed all day."

He hooked my hair behind my ears. "I want you to take off your earrings," he said. The earrings in question were tiny gold studs a little bigger than a pin head. "I don't want you to have anything on."

I said, "Will you stay home with a debilitating disease?"

Patrick said, "I'm going to call up and say I've died and gone to heaven."

It rained all Monday and we only left the house once, for five minutes, to buy *The New York Times*. Not even rapture got in the way of that.

I said, "If you did die and go to heaven, I bet you'd stop and buy the *Times*."

"I always buy the *Times*," said Patrick. "But now I'm in love with it."

He looked like the man who invented ease, and we were both genuinely happy. I was not waiting for any crash, or for some grim insight to take its toll: this all felt perfectly right to me. We found ourselves in a glut of usable riches, which we compounded, and by the afternoon, worn out by our affection, we took a nap. We had kept a fire going in the bedroom fireplace all day, and as Patrick slept I watched the embers in that dark room. He lay beside me wrapped in a plaid car rug. The Baxes' cars and guest rooms always had a plaid wool blanket neatly folded. They could not have napped without one. When he turned slightly in his sleep, the rug slipped off his shoulder and I could not bear to cover him up without putting my cheek next to his flesh. He smelled like cooked sugar, and his heart beat as steadily as a steel watch.

It seemed to me, as I watched the glow die in the hearth, that there was daily life, and there was the secret heart of things. Daily life would find me and Patrick and the rest of the world taking showers, going to work, and planning out the details of living. The details Patrick seemed most eager to streamline were the elements of a groundplan that would keep us together in some gentle, close, unquestioned way, as if he felt that to talk things over was to have everything explode at once. He said he had been caught off guard by happiness. He said he had not expected any real joy in his life, but he had prepped for it, anyway.

In that moment of sweet comfort, I wondered about the history of our secret hearts. When Patrick was still my brother-in-law, I had counted on him, not for any sustenance, but because I knew I was intelligible to him in a way I was not to Sam. I had never wondered then if I loved him. He wasn't mine to love, but he was someone in my immediate landscape whom I treasured. Now we were presuming on an untried intimacy, and we were frightened by it. In some parts of the world, it was incest we were committing, and daily life, if we continued together, meant Meridia and Leonard and my parents, a series of raised eyebrows and disapproving telephone calls.

But the secret heart of things was the ground I stood on. What arrangements people construct in the name of love are as formal and artful as any other product of human devotion. You figured them out as you went along, with an eye toward grace, as if you were writing a sonata, and the sense that propelled you was the goodness of the thing. My feelings for Patrick propelled me along. I didn't want their history explained to me. I didn't want to know if Patrick, at Little Crab, or in Cambridge, or some night at the Baxes' had fallen into love, and I didn't want to ask myself what set of intricate baby steps had led me to what I felt was so inalienably right. It didn't matter.

When Patrick woke up, we watched the evening news and had our dinner, after which Patrick looked over a brief and read a mystery entitled *The Serpent in the Suitcase*. He read with fierce concentration.

"Who wrote that thing?" I said.

"Shut up," said Patrick.

"What's the title of it?"

"I don't know. Leave me alone. There's a water moccasin wrapped around the shower curtain."

It took him forty-five minutes to read it, after which we

drank hot toddys and watched a late-night movie called *The Terror*, another mystery Patrick was hot to watch. It concerned a pair of French aristocrats being kept prisoner in their own château by a flock of men wearing ski masks, speaking to one another in badly synched English. "Give this gun to me, or I shall have to blow your guts out," said the largest of the masked men. We turned it off and went to bed.

We slept the sleep of the just and innocent, that sweet sleep you keep waking from then drift back into. After our long weekend, we treated each other with exaggerated but gentle respect, as if marking the boundaries of our separate privacy in order to see them more clearly. But still, we couldn't stay apart for very long.

XV I didn't want to love Patrick: I didn't know how to go about it. I knew all about leaping into love, about getting carried away, about jumps of faith and flashes of intuition. I knew about chance and dare and lust and the love of risk it takes to get into a car with Richard Cruise. But I didn't know anything about the slow approach, the accumulation of admiration, the long slide into the depths of love. I believed that if you connected, you went off like a flashbulb. I didn't know anything at all about patience, and it seemed to me that no matter with what stealth you approached passion, no matter how long the waiting time spins out before it erupts, it is the soul of impatience, and recklessness lives right in the heart of it.

I thought that although I hadn't plotted for Sam, I had waited all my life for someone like him. Sam tied up the whole package. My feelings for Patrick functioned out of another set of rules in a game I was new to, whose order was dim to me. We slipped into a slightly chaotic but definitely domestic routine. After all, I had been domesticated for quite a while, and Patrick had been hoping for the shape his life was assuming. We were too grown up for snipings in the dark, hysterical telephone calls, cryptic messages, and we had known each other too long for clashing histories and misunderstandings. So we didn't undergo what emerging lovers have to bear, but it was only superficially that we were the other's most convenient choice. The fact is, we were a perfect match. We had the same fondness for order, for quietude, we had the same deep streak of intensity running through us, and we savored it in the same way. We went to concerts. We went to the movies. We went dancing at a big, slummy joint called Penny's Paradise. Basically, we hung around, divided equally between my apartment, where the piano was, and Patrick's, where his papers were.

Our privacy, our quietude, our mutual propriety kept the world at bay for a time. We were working on feeling, not talking about it. Being lovers had rearranged our friendship and superseded the bond we were used to. But above us, like a bright, high cloud with a dark side, floated the idea of Sam, causing me and Patrick to do battle with a strong sense of sin. Had he been coveting his brother's wife? And had his brother's wife been keeping a secret eye out for him? But Patrick hadn't coveted me. He had been stumped by my presence in Sam's company, and he had never thought Sam and I would end up together. In the hardheadedness of my loyalty to Sam I had thought, but never noticed, how difficult it was to be married to him. But it didn't matter, except that Patrick and I didn't want the issue of us confused. We didn't want to fall into some awful mistake, so for a while we made a mutual pact to rack up as much pleasure as we could with the least amount of intrusion.

You can suspend thought, but you can't stop yourself from thinking. I wondered how much Sam there was latent in Patrick and he wondered how much revenge on Sam there was in his choice of me. We were right to wonder and we were not shy about asking, but there was a real possibility of turning Sam into an obsession; we wanted to see how deep our bond went without him.

Joining with Patrick was no accident caused by rain and whiskey. The event itself was a surprise, as all events are, but not the fact of it. The fact of it was as natural as the weather. Once past the fact, we were only two people who knew each other, up to a point.

Sam's rebelliousness had made him accident prone: he was all surfaces, and his waywardness was as apparent as the sling on his arm. Patrick dealt in depth charges. Sam was a lawyer because it was the easiest and smoothest thing for him to be—because Leonard was and because Cyrus Bax had been. Sam liked to discuss cases with Leonard. It was another form of tennis for them both. But, as Henry Jacobs said, Patrick's connection to the law was passionate, and this passion was unintelligible to Leonard, with whom he never discussed anything. Life to Sam was matter, and to Patrick it was the mind over it. Waywardness in Patrick led to slaps in the face of this kind—the son who wouldn't speak, the son who would take up his father's profession and never talk shop, the son who had made himself, by virtue of constant, cautionary lessons, what his parents were not, while Sam was the caricature of what they were. Patrick lay back. His manners were flawless. He hadn't flipped out, shot heroin, or lived in a truck. He was a son you could take around in company. But, underneath, the priorities of his life had been arranged away from anything Leonard or Meridia had to offer, and his life was spent in vigilance against what he was heir to: that cold, offhand, tunnel-visioned amputation of the heart and soul the Baxes had undergone and never, never rued.

The first few months we were together I could not get over the feeling that I was being given the key to a locked room containing secreted treasures. Patrick gave me access and it wasn't easy for him, but it was what he wanted. There is privacy, there is remoteness, and there is the stand you take about privacy. Patrick believed that a confidence was an honor conferred in friendship, and so did I. Sam blurted, but he was as remote as his mother, that stylish flint wall. I had known Sam as well as he could be known, I thought with grief, but the key to his locked room was lost even to him. He hadn't had much in the way of an emotional vocabulary and when he said he loved me it was true, but it was only a fact, like Meridia's domestic arrangements. Loving me made life easier for him. It got him off the hook of life. Having said it, there was nothing more to be done. Sam was complicated, all right, but he didn't care.

But Patrick was a miracle of rare device. He was the precision machine that contemplates with interest the workings of its own parts. He was a great speculator; he was a distinction-maker. In his bottom drawer was a file of clippings cut from the newspapers and I often thought if I could find out the lowest common denominator of those clippings I would have known him all at once: family murders, faith healers, bogus stock issues, the history of the Albanian community in the Bronx, the scandal of Tipica College, which gave out divinity degrees if you sent in twenty-five dollars and your blood type and a pledge that you had never had any alcoholic beverage, the death of a race horse at the three-quarter-mile pole. There was a grand private design to these, known only to Patrick.

Having him tell you the plot of one of his mysteries was better than reading it, and I used to make him tell me the plots of movies I had seen, just to hear him. For Patrick, there was a plot beneath the plot—he called it underplot—and he could knock off the story in a couple of sentences. What he liked was what got the thing going. He was a big fan of tone and gesture, those nuances you could fix on sixty different ways. If he had not been so capable of delight, his interest in detail would have approached the sinister. But life did delight him, in all its moving parts. He sat back and watched the world plot and move and shift. In public he was slightly shy, but he was charmed by what people thought, or thought they thought, and what they did unthinkingly. Patrick found odd sides on even the dullest citizen. If he had not had a nasty side, if he had not had a small streak of natural mimic, he might have approached sanctity. But he also had a temper.

Patrick angered on a slow burn. His propriety was such that shouting or on-the-spot hostilities were impossible for him, so he took proper stock of what annoyed him and who had wronged him and saved it up until his anger burned through, and then he was prone to incandescent rages, but they were only flash fires—hot and brief. You knew what he disapproved of only by the flicker of disgust that ran across his eyes. When I first met him, the word for him was lofty. From the perch of his high horse, he looked down on the rest of the world and judged harshly, and while he had once been fury waiting for an outlet, he had calmed down as he got older. There was still a fiery keenness about him, but his life was no longer a struggle for mildness against vehemence. He was not so vehement as he had thought, nor was he so addicted to mildness as he had once believed. But he was a good solid hater when he wanted to be, and his hates, which he kept sharpened, were all ancient history: a professor he had wanted to murder, and a colleague in his first law firm. He never saw either of these people, but he liked to keep his hate intact, so from time to time he would trot it out, and I would get fifteen minutes of pure invective.

The list of things he liked or loved or craved was endless. He was in fact quite easy to please. He wanted coffee ice cream all the time and you could make him happy with any book about birds or snakes. He loved mystery novels, which he bought, read, and threw away, and he liked what he called "German twilight fiction"—Brosch, Storm, and Robert Musil. The movies he admired were in color, had a lot of love interest and very little social content—a really bloody Western or some unbelievably tear-jerking romance. As a child he had filled his cupboards with rocks and minerals, and his collection, a modified edition thereof, was still with him. When you walked on the beach with Patrick, you noticed that he walked with his head down. Some of his collection dotted the mantelpiece in his bedroom, and some of it was used for paperweights. If you asked him he could tell you where each was from, and on what walk in what town in East Anglia he had found his lump of red flint.

He loved clocks, and in the back of his closet was a box of old watch parts he had bought for a dollar in Maine. He had inherited Cyrus Bax's grandfather clock, which had painted on its lid a four-rigger, and from Meridia's mother an alabaster clock on top of which sat a brooding bronze griffin. On his desk was a blue plastic elephant clock with the face in its stomach, the clock that had been a childhood gift. None of these clocks told the right time. For that you went into the bedroom, where he kept a cheap white electric alarm clock that did not ring but rasped you out of sleep.

He liked to be read to, and he liked to read out loud. He liked to buy the early edition of *The New York Times* and read it before he went to bed. He liked beer and he liked to go to the races, and he watched basketball on television, since his firm—to his great sorrow—didn't have seats at the Garden. He liked to putter around when he was thinking, and his artistic ambitions were confined to a set of watercolors he dragged out one rainy evening. We sat head to head under a high-intensity lamp, painting a clumsy, primary-colored, visually illiterate edition of a unicorn tapestry, which Patrick had framed and hung over the bed. The unicorn, a joint effort, had one blue eye and one faintly green one, of two different shapes. He looked somewhat goatlike, and his horn was striped blue and yellow and red. In the background were a pack of dogs that looked like boulders with cat faces, but the wildflowers were very precise.

If we were at my apartment, he liked to listen to me practice and he made me play the pieces I had written; he paced while he listened, his hands locked behind him like a cartoon edition of a German philosopher. Although we cohabited with real sweetness and our intentions at the time were blockheaded and direct as we fended the world off, those first few months were difficult once our mutual amazement wore off. First of all, it was hard to push things aside, although we knew we were right to. It was hard to establish an easy rhythm between us—after all, we were strangers keeping house. And it was hard to maintain that calculated innocence. It made us slightly fragile. As a result, Patrick got the flu and had to stay home for three days. He propped himself up with pillows, looking haggard and boyish, reading *The New York Times* and watching soap operas on the television. He was sweet and fevered and bored. When I came home, we played scrabble and then a card game he and Sam had made up and played since childhood called "Killer Swaps," whose rules were ridiculous and complicated. This amused him nicely for an hour, and then he napped. When he woke up, he feebly gulped down pints of coffee ice cream, the only thing he wanted to eat besides buttered toast. His fever made him mellow and sentimental, and when I got up early on a wet, bitter day to go out and get him the paper I had to fling it on the bed and stalk out for fear he would weep with gratitude.

When he got well, I got sick. I hadn't been sick since childhood, and the brand of flu I got gave me a fever so low grade that I woke up one morning with hands and feet and bones so cold I thought I had died during the night. Patrick got me out of bed, sat me down in front of a fire, and changed the bedding. Being sick made me despair.

When I looked at myself in the mirror, I was the color of ash, but when the worst was over and I began to look less like a corpse, Patrick made me a formal dinner. He covered the table with a cloth that must have been Meridia's. He was a precise, good cook: this was the meal to welcome me back to the world of the living, and he watched over me with a solicitude that made me weepy. Over dessert, I broke down, sobbing apologies.

Patrick said, "After a death in the family, everyone gets sick."

I said, "I want to talk about Sam."

"So do I," said Patrick.

"My instinct tells me that the way I feel about you doesn't have anything to do with him, but that can't be the truth."

"My instinct tells me that you don't have anything to do with him, in the way I feel, but I believe it."

"It can't be."

"It can and it can't," said Patrick. "There are some nasty facts in this matter. What's going on now couldn't have happened if Sam hadn't died. I didn't want him to die, but he did. I know that in the back of my mind I've held you as something I've wanted for years, but I never would have done anything about it, and I never hoped that Sam would fade away. I thought you two would divorce, and I wondered what I'd do if you did."

"But you thought we would."

"Listen, Elizabeth. I don't have any love for the members of my family. Leonard's all right. He's a good father for a five-year-old boy. Meridia is all right too, but they're the coldest fish this side of the South Pole. I loved Sam probably the way you did. He was great to watch, but you know how fixed his limits were. In family matters, my family is all alike. They hang together like icicles. I wondered how long you could keep on being what you manifestly are in that company."

"Where do you fit in?"

"I'm their opposite. The wonderful thing about Leonard and Meridia is how little keeps them pleased. They like to keep the lid on. Sam liked to blow the lid off. I'm not interested in lids. I'm their odd duck."

He was their odd duck, all right, their swan, their eagle, the heron that stood brooding and reflecting in a still pool. That was the first of our discussions about the Baxes: I was a Bax, too, technically. We discussed these things in short takes, over a long time. But the rest of the time we put our hands over our eyes, with only a space between our fingers to see the other. Both of those stances, we felt, were right. We would have been silly if we had not been so serious, so dedicated to caution, so careful to see if we were right, since we both felt our position to be risky and assailable. What would the world say about us, we sinning in-laws? Couldn't a case be made for the plotting of the thing? Didn't it look just too convenient for words? It would have been a falsity not to have thought these things through, so we thought them. But Patrick and I knew what a pair of *ponderosos* we could be, and there was too much joy in us to be denied. Everyone in love is foolish, so we trotted around like a pair of perfectly matched fools. We were also fools for order.

Patrick was almost as fastidious as Meridia, but not for the sake of dispensing with things. Order saved time, he thought, but in matters of the heart—the explosive matter of our communal heart—it was correctness he wanted and so did I. Order in the world created comfort for Patrick, and his apartment was a cross between a neat boy's room and Meridia's study. There was no place you couldn't comfortably sprawl or shut yourself off if you needed to. We spent stretches of our time together in peaceful quietude. Together, we got a lot of work done. Sam had been too frenetic to read in the same room with. The piano bothered him, and in order to study he had to lock himself away. If he couldn't find a place in Widener Library, he holed himself up in the bicycle room of our apartment building.

Patrick liked to unfold on his couch. I curled into his big striped chair. On these laps of comfort, we read the hours away. It was a pleasure to look up from the page, turn my head, and see Patrick absorbed in his mysteries, his twilight fiction, his bird and snake books. He was a reactive reader: he laughed out loud, groaned, and snorted. When he hit a passage that set him off, he looked over politely and then read it to me.

He was neat, but he had pockets of real sloppiness. He didn't like to see a chair out of place and a slightly crooked painting drove him crazy, but on his dresser was a huge glass ashtray into which he dumped the pennies his jacket pocket was always filled with. This ashtray was so full it spilled when you opened the top drawer. In the morning the floor was littered with pennies. His camera was safe in its case and the negatives were neatly filed, but the prints were stacked haphazardly in a tattered interoffice envelope. In one tiny closet, whose door had to be forced, Patrick had established a little spot of chaos. In it were crammed several unstrung tennis rackets, the set of watercolors, a broken ski, several torn sweaters, a couple of tarnished trophies, hiking boots, a carton of dusty term papers, his rock and mineral collection, a pith helmet, a large box containing his income tax statements, loose tennis balls, and a Malacca cane—relic of Cyrus Bax—that was decorated with dancing skeletons.

Sometimes, if he left before me in the morning, I would wander around his apartment as if I had come to another planet by affectionate invitation. There were times when I pushed the jammed door of that closet open and stood looking into the jumble as if it were the middens of Troy. There were the artifacts of an entirely different life and the sight of his discarded toys gave me a turn. It seemed to me that no matter how long you lived with men—no matter how long you lived with a man—there were things that reminded you that they were totally unlike women. But then, it wasn't men and women: it was me and Patrick. It was the heady sense with which you come to people you love—as if they were the history of Western civilization, full of shrines, museums, battles, monuments, churches, and arrowheads.

When, in a moment of true soupiness, I revealed to Patrick that I had stood in front of this closet with tears in my eyes, he told me that when he discovered that I kept lavender soap in with my sweaters he had felt slightly dizzy, as if he had found a secret letter.

All that rainy summer, I worked for Max at Butler Library. When the weather was fine, Patrick and I took off for the weekend to the beach, but not to Little Crab. It was the first year Patrick did not go up—we were waiting to go together and present ourselves to Leonard and Meridia as a pair. Meanwhile, we made nothing public, and we kept low, but we were positively prancing with good health. There are decisions your flesh makes for you, and we could not deny the visible evidence that we had struck some rich vein of happiness: the flesh carries on a happy, mindless life of its own.

In late August, I was to go away to the Hamilton Conservatory for a month, and Patrick had to be in Washington and California, so we spent the summer consolidating. Before I left, I put my furniture into storage, except for the piano, which was moved on a stifling day to Patrick's, along with my clothes, books, scores, and sentimental objects. We decided that when we both got back we would move, and then we would begin our perilous trek to Boston to confront the Baxes and to Old Lyme to confront the Marcuses, and we would have Henry Jacobs for dinner.

But there were days when I thought I would die, days when

my hold on Sam—a hold I had grown used to and counted on, that I had substituted for my hold of grief—was so tenuous and far away I felt I had lost a hold on myself. Sam was my first language, the mother tongue I referred back to in my sleep or when caught off guard. I was losing it, and it seemed too soon to lose it. I felt like a murderess or a betrayer. It was too much to think about, but nothing stopped it. When I sifted my affections and measured my feelings, I knew that in most ways my feelings about Patrick had nothing to do with Sam. Only in most ways, but there were others.

My days with Sam were finally over, and I was frightened. Sam was a pip. Sam was a hoot. Sam was haywire. When I thought of Sam, and I saw how much my vision had changed, I felt like a true criminal of the heart. Energy was not passion: Sam had the one, but Patrick had them both. Part of Sam's appeal was that you could never figure out if he had been spoiled or deprived. Anything you gave him thrilled him, anything you didn't pained him. He kept himself safe that way. But Patrick made you feel he had been spoiled with the things he didn't much care about and deprived of the things he valued, and he had carved out a life he valued, while Sam threw his away.

I was still mourning, and that made me feel toward Patrick a fierce tenderness: he was grieving too. That knowledge complicated things. I was no longer mourning on my own and I did not want us to be caught in some ritual undercurrent, tied together by a boating accident or bound by a freak storm.

There was more life, and Patrick was it. As the days passed, Sam got to be more and more a photograph. The thought that someone I had loved so much had passed into memory was bitter, bitter and appalling. I saw Sam as I would have seen him through the wrong end of a telescope at fifty paces on the beach. He was so close he was almost upon me, but when I looked, he stood at the end of a great expanse, so diminished I could hardly make him out, so small I could have put him neatly in my scrapbook.

PART III

PART II

XVI My first night in Hamilton, New Hampshire, a seventeen-year-old Canadian genius named Giles Bronner played Brahms intermezzi. He was a tall, gaunt boy with angry red hair. When he looked up from the keys, the expression on his face was a cross between rapture and goofiness, and in the more intense moments, he threw back his head and dropped his lower lip, giving him the look of a slack-jawed, beatified moron, but he played like an angel. The little hall in which he performed had once been a chapel—a gray and white chapel—with bare pine pews and painted beams. Under the great Bechstein slept a golden retriever that belonged to the caretaker and his wife.

According to the booklet I found lying on my night table, the grounds of the Hamilton Conservatory had once been a Quaker boys' school, which, upon folding in 1895, had been purchased by Thaddeus McCane, a railroad magnate and horse breeder who added to the stark clapboard school buildings several elaborate Victorian houses, a stable so huge it had been converted by the Conservatory into an administration building and dining hall, and a round Shaker barn that was now used as a snack bar and common room, furnished in Palm Beach wicker. When McCane died, the family had leased the property to a Protestant ecumenical group, which held meetings and retreats, and had built the chapel and several one-room cottages—now rehearsal halls. This architectural mix, painted a uniform gray and trimmed in white, was set in a valley surrounded by wooded mountains. At midday the sun poured down on the gray gables, dazzling you, and on cloudy days it looked as if the buildings had been painted the precise color of an overcast sky.

I had arrived too late for dinner, but was given a cup of coffee and a doughnut by Theo Zeller, the director. After I registered I was shown to my room in one of the cottages—a former dormitory—by Laura Zeller, Theo's daughter, a plump sixteen-year-old with white-gold braids and petulant sulk. She pointed me in the direction of the chapel so that I could find my way to Giles Bronner after I unpacked.

The night cloaked everything and the lights from the chapel gleamed out of the darkness. I sat in the back row during the concert looking at the heads of a group of strangers. After the performance I was too tired and shy to socialize. The only person I could have located was Theo Zeller, but he had disappeared, and Laura Zeller was standing by the piano, patting the awakened dog. I found my way back to my room alone and fell asleep.

The next morning, the light woke me, and I took a long walk before breakfast in order to get a feel of the place by myself. The campus lay soft and bright in the early sun. I stuck to the side of the main road and kept my eye on the surrounding woods and fields to get the lay of the land. I walked four miles down the road, and on my way back I saw a large man in a sweat suit jogging across a field. He had thick dark hair that flopped in his face. When he saw me, he jogged in my direction and finally stood before me, blocking my path. He had an open, slightly bullish face and the body of an aging football player that he was trying to maintain against odds. He looked about forty, puffing furiously and dripping wet.

"We're the only people up," he said when he had caught his breath.

"I like to have the morning to myself," I said. "How many miles do you jog?"

"Three. How many miles do you walk?"

"Eight."

"Admirable," he said. He had a smile of incomparable

sweetness and it came over his sweating, scowling features slowly and left a trace of itself at the corners of his mouth. He had dimples and a rich voice with the remnants of a drawl.

"I'm Charlie Pepper," he said, extending his large hand.

"I'm Elizabeth Bax."

"Well, Elizabeth. You have one of the smallest hands I've ever clutched."

We walked back together and he told me that he was a pediatrician from Knoxville and that he played second cello in the symphony.

"They keep me on for my curiosity value, but I come up here to make sure they don't fire me. I'm the tallest person in the symphony and the only doctor." He asked me what had brought me to the Conservatory and I told him that I played the piano, that I was researching for a book, and that I had been away from musical people for a long time.

He said, "Some afternoon will you play duets with me?"

"I'm out of practice. I haven't played with anyone for a year."

"Honey," he said, "you haven't heard anything until you hear an oversized aging baby doctor like myself sawing away."

At the edge of the campus, he showed me where he was putting up, in one of Thaddeus McCane's Victorian houses, and said he would see me at breakfast. He smiled his lovely smile and I saw that he wore around his neck a dull chain bearing a disk. Up close it had engraved upon it two crossed snakes stamped in red and a warning that the wearer was fatally allergic to penicillin.

Breakfast was at eight-thirty so very few people showed up for it. I sat with Theo Zeller, Charlie Pepper, and Laura Zeller. Theo was an old friend of Max Price's and we talked about him until Mrs. Zeller—Anna—appeared with the morning papers. We drank our coffee and read in silence.

By the end of the day, I had visited the library, walked four more miles, and eaten two meals. Under the trees, around the pond, on the creeper-covered porches, students and musicians were talking earnestly or taking the sun. Someone was playing the violin in one of the rehearsal halls as I walked by. I had had time to observe that Laura Zeller and Giles Bronner were in love, and this was verified by Charlie Pepper, who had spent five summers at the conservatory. At lunchtime their eyes were very glazed and sleepy, and I suspected that Laura and Giles took off time to smoke reefer in the woods.

Before dinner I did the rest of my unpacking. My cottage had once housed eight Quaker boys. Now it held four women: me, an elderly German named Elsa Costello (her late husband was Irish), who was writing a biography of Michael Haydn, a nun from Cincinnati who taught at a Sacred Heart college, and Libby Hayes, a harpsichordist from London with the strong, determined hands of a strangler.

A great wave of shyness had overtaken me, and I approached meals with something very like terror. Suppose the Zellers didn't want me at their table? Laura and Giles spoke only to each other. Wasn't I intruding? The staff all knew one another; a large percentage of people were summer regulars, and the students had school in common. I didn't fit at all.

I paused at the door before dinner, but as I stood, two hands closed around my elbow and I looked up at Charlie Pepper.

"I've come to appropriate you," he said. "You sit by me."

After dinner, there was nothing to do until the eight o'clock performance. If you wandered around, you heard someone practicing the flute, you heard scales being played on a bassoon, and from the round barn, a Mozart sonata for four hands.

It was dusk. You could see the last thin line of a pink sunset lowering itself down the side of a mountain. I sat on a stone bench in the middle of what had been the Quaker boys' playing field and talked to Charlie Pepper, who described the social workings of the place. After the night performance you could go, if you were invited, to the Zellers' house down the road and get politely drunk. Or you could sit around the barn drinking coffee in front of a fire. Or else you had a party in your room, or got invited to one. Or if you were Laura and

Giles, you found a comfortable, out-of-the-way copse in which to get stoned. One of the cottages near the dining hall was run like a country club: you stashed your bottle there with your name on it, and a cheerful student functioned as bartender. If you were bored and had a car, you could go off the grounds. The most popular place was a bar in Milford Haven, four miles away, but Charlie's spot was a seedy bar and grill in the minuscule town of Shortford.

When the eight o'clock bell rang, Charlie and I walked toward the chapel to hear Libby Hayes play the Goldberg Variations. Afterward, I was at loose ends, invaded again by shyness. I told Charlie I was going back to my room.

"I'm real sorry to hear that," he said.

"It takes me a while to get used to a place," I said.

"Don't let it take too long."

By the end of the first week everyone had arrived and I was used to the pace. Each morning I got up early to take my walk, and as I came up the road Charlie would jog across the field so we could walk to breakfast together. I found myself beside him at most meals, and whenever he sat at another table, I felt a little disconnected. Laura and Giles had decided, apparently, that I was not too horrible to acknowledge, so when I didn't sit with Charlie I sat with them.

But until I got my real bearings, I hid out in the library on the ground floor of one of the Victorian houses. The chairs were ratty and comfortable, slightly damp when you settled into them. There was a bookcase of scores, a long shelf of records next to a stereo with head sets, file drawers of letters— composers and musicians connected with the conservatory left their papers to it—and a collection of monographs on American music. When you looked up from your work, you saw rolling lawns dipping into woods that led up the sides of the hills.

I stuck to the library, to Laura and Giles, and to Charlie, when he was not socializing elsewhere. Laura was plump and creamy. When she was abstracted, she wove and unwove her plait. She wore bluejeans and old-fashioned blouses embroidered with flowers and she dealt with her parents as if she were a prisoner of war—sullen, but polite. She and Giles pulled their chairs close together at meals, and Giles kept his bony arms close to his sides while he ate in order not to elbow her away from him.

In the evenings, I went to the Zellers', or to the barn for coffee. I spent a few evenings drinking with Charlie Pepper, who revealed to me that he was forty-three, that he had a wife named Mary Beth, three children, a water spaniel, and a fifteen-pound cat whose name was Tiny. He had been born and raised in Knoxville, but he had spent eight years in Canada getting educated at McGill.

So I settled in. The women I shared the cottage with were brisk and cheerful and considerate with the hot water in the shower. I was used to seeing Charlie, used to sitting with him at the Zellers'.

One morning I was accosted by Laura Zeller before lunch. "Giles asked me to talk to you," she said. "He likes you."

"I'm honored."

"Most people don't understand Giles very well," she said. "He doesn't get along with adults, but he thinks that's immature. You're a sort of borderline case, so he and I thought you might come down to the pond with us tonight."

"To help Giles reconcile himself with the adult word?"

"Well, Giles and I don't meet all that many people up here that we like, and we like you. We're just going to smoke a little dope and sit around."

"Would you like some wine, if I bring it?"

"Sure," said Laura. "Right after the concert."

I met them by the pond at ten o'clock with a bottle of white wine and a clothesline. We tied up the bottle and put it in the pond to cool and Giles produced a clay pipe. While the wine cooled, we smoked a little dope, which glowed in the darkness as we passed it around. You could hear the pop of frogs jumping in the pond, and the crickets and mourning doves.

We stretched out on the grass and I told them how glad I was they had invited me.

"Most people are insane pigs," said Giles. He had his arm around Laura, who had unbraided her hair and pushed it over one shoulder. Their faces were filled with innocence and hostility; a clear case of teenage them-against-us-ism, banded together as they were against the world.

When we thought the wine had cooled sufficiently, we passed the bottle. Giles reloaded his pipe. You could smell the watery, earthy scent of the pond, and the crickets threw up a solid wall of sound.

"We come down here to cool out," said Laura.

"We come down here to get away from all those insane pigs," said Giles. "That's why we asked you. You look placid, but not stupid."

"You are an adolescent monster, Giles," I said.

"That's true," he said.

"You shouldn't say that to him," said Laura.

"That's okay," said Giles. "Anything that's true is okay. She was probably an adolescent monster herself."

We were quiet for a while, and then Laura began to sing. She sang an old Otis Redding song called "That's How Strong My Love Is," and she sang it in an ardent, dreamy voice. Giles dropped his head onto her shoulder and I sat with my arms locked around my legs.

> I'll be the weeping willow drowning in my tears
> And you can go swimming whenever you are near
> And I'll be the rainbow after the tears are gone
> To wrap you in my colors and keep you warm.

She sang the same verse three times. Her voice echoed slightly.

"I love Otis Redding," Giles said.

"So do I," said Laura, dreamily. They seemed locked forever, and had I not been so high, I would have felt that bond exclusionary. Instead, it drew me to them. I moved a little closer. Laura began to sing again, and then we all sang. Giles had a throaty, squeaky voice.

I'll be the moon when the sun goes down
Just to let you know that I'm still around.
That's how strong my love is, that's how strong my love is.

When we stopped, I saw that we were sitting in a circle and that we were holding hands. The moon appeared from behind a cloud and we blinked in the sudden, soft brightness. They moved closer together and I knew it was time to leave them alone. We smiled fuzzily, and I kissed them both goodnight.

As I crossed the road to my cottage, I saw Charlie Pepper walking toward his room and I thought to call to him but didn't. The light in my room was out, and I didn't put it on. I lay beneath the scratchy sheets, a cool breeze on my neck, humming myself to sleep.

XVII My room smelled of camomile and mown grass. The library smelled of pine and varnish and had large, curved windows against which grew a species of prehistoric fern. In front of one of the windows was a drooping spruce. When the light came in, it came in green, but a space amidst the foliage let in a charge of pure sunlight that illuminated a spot of worn-out carpet. The day after my night with Laura and Giles I stayed in the library, drinking coffee and working.

Late in the afternoon, I took a stroll through the woods to stretch my legs and heard the music of a cello. I walked toward one of the rehearsal halls, but when I got there, the music had stopped. The little quarters looked like something out of Grimm—some dotty architect's notion of spatial solitude—with peaked roofs and diminutive windows. I looked in and saw Charlie Pepper sitting in the middle of that empty whitewashed room. The floor had been varnished Colonial orange and the whole room glowed with it. It was near sundown and a stripe of pink light came through the west window. His bow rested across his knees. He was huge beside the cello, like a big man on a little horse. It had been a hot day and he had his pocket kerchief tied around his neck.

He picked up his bow and began to play the Saraband from the Sixth Cello Suite, with beautiful deliberation. I leaned my elbows against the window ledge and took a deep breath. It seemed just that such a big man should produce such a deep

147

sound, that the room should be flooded with sunset, that he should have around his throat a yellow-and-blue bandana. The back of his shirt was wet. He stopped and put the bow across his knees and when he began to play again, I walked away. It wasn't just practice for him—it was obviously a private moment and I didn't want to peer invisibly at it. As I walked back, the music followed me.

I ambled though the woods, past a stand of birches to a stream, where I sat on a rock and watched the water running past me. Then I ran across the field. When I got to my room, flushed and out of breath, Charlie Pepper was standing in the doorway.

"Where were you last night?" he said. "Where were you today?"

"I was down at the pond getting high last night and today I was in the library."

"I looked all over for you," he said.

"Well, you didn't look in the right places."

"I looked *everywhere*." He glared at me with pure accusation, which I took to be a form of tease.

I said, "You've found me, so what's the difference?"

He said, "I'm in love with you."

"Don't be so silly."

"I'm not being silly. I'm being serious."

"Listen," I said. "You don't know me and you're seven times my size, so knock it off."

He sat down on the bed.

"You New York girls have no heart," he said. "I heard you singing down by the pond."

"That was Laura Zeller."

"That was *you*. I could tell it was you when the three of you were singing together."

"Why didn't you make your presence known?"

"I didn't think you teenagers would want a great beast of the wilderness crashing in on you."

"I watched you play this afternoon," I said.

"Was I any good?"

"You were terrific."

148

"Then kiss me as my reward."

I said, "You Knoxville doctors are spoiled brats."

"It won't kill an honorable girl like yourself to kiss a man in need."

I bent down and kissed him on the mouth. He smiled.

"You're supposed to turn into Gregor Piatigorski," I said.

"I'm just Good Time Charlie Pepper," he said. "Now. My motive for being in your room is to tell you that I've done a little research on you, and I'm told you have a car. Will you allow me to drive it and you down the road apiece to get a decent meal?"

I fished in my bag and tossed him the keys. He caught them left-handed. "Half an hour," he said. "In the parking lot."

Before I met him, I stopped by the library and got two scores for the Brahms E Minor cello and piano sonata. Charlie scrutinized it in the car.

"This'll kill me," he said.

"It's always wise to overreach."

"Well, aren't you the primmest thing since shredded wheat," he said.

"I don't think that's a fit way to talk to a girl you're in love with."

He started the car. "It's never wise to mock at something you're too flippant and suspicious to accept."

"I don't like being teased."

"You're a serious girl," said Charlie. "I have no recourse but to get you drunk."

We drove into the twilight down a crooked road that followed a creek.

"If you sit any farther away, you're going to fall out of the car," Charlie said. "There are a lot of hairpin turns on this road."

I slid over next to him and he put his arm around me.

I said, "Aren't you the ardent teen."

"I'm the ardent adult," he said.

We drove to a roadhouse in Milford Haven, a whitewashed Colonial house with a neon beer sign in the window. It was the home of the best smothered chicken in the north, Charlie claimed. We were the only people in the restaurant, but at the bar were a pair of sleepy-looking locals. Charlie ordered two double bourbons and drank half of his in a gulp.

"Your car isn't the only thing I've found out about you," he said.

"It's one of the more interesting."

"You're a widow," he said, drawling out the word.

I sipped my drink, amazed at how unsteady my voice felt.

"That just about wraps me up," I said. "Now you can tell me how sad it is and we can have a good old weep."

"Don't be defensive," he said. "It's only a condition. You don't appear to be a tragic figure."

"It isn't tragic. It's just hard on you."

"Well, I'm sympathetic to that," he said, and took my hand.

Over dinner, he told me about Mary Beth. They had been grammar school sweethearts, and then she had moved away. They found each other again at McGill by what they considered miraculous coincidence. She wrote children's books and was, he said, his lifeline. From his wallet he produced a picture of his children: Charles Jr., who was ten; Nell, eight; and Andrew, a three-year-old with enormous eyes.

"Mary Beth is the rock on which I stand," he said. "But my flesh is weak and I fall in love. Not very often, and when I do, it's usually a mistake. It doesn't last long but it puts a little fire into my life, although it doesn't shake the bond. But you are something else again. Something else entirely."

I said, "You Southerners are deeply specious."

He grabbed me by the arm. "Don't you know when you're being told something, you doltish woman?"

"I know when I'm being flirted with."

"I'm not flirting," Charlie said. "You haven't any faith, but you'll learn." He poured us both another glass of beer. "Now let's even things up," he said. "Who were you married to, and what happened to him?"

I told him about Sam. I described him, since there was nothing I could pull out of my wallet to show. I hadn't looked at a picture of Sam since his death, and it pained me to think

150

that the day would come when I could face that mound of photographs again.

After dinner, Charlie lit a cigar and ordered brandy. By the time the place closed, he was as drunk as a skunk.

"Gimme the keys. You're not fit to sit behind the wheel," I said.

"Only if you put out in the back seat."

"I'm not even putting out in the front seat."

He gave me the keys with a great grin, but when we got into the car, he stopped grinning. He put his arms around me and kissed me.

"You're a very restrained woman," he said.

"I'm not a restrained woman, but I'm not sure what I'm doing. I don't want to be a tease."

"I can see how you'd be sensitive on that issue," he said.

"You put me in this position."

"Then don't come at me with Brahms sonatas."

"Well, don't take anything as a come on."

He leaned against the door looking mournful, and my heart gave way. After a week of chat with strangers, he was the one person I didn't want to keep strange. My instinct told me I was right to want to know him, and hadn't I always put my trust in instinct? Didn't I believe in friendship at first sight? We were knocking out the lines of friendship and the form it took was flirting.

I said, "I like you a lot, Charlie."

"Is that a considered statement?"

"It's instinct."

"Good," he said. "Let's go back now. I'll walk you to the door of your little shack, but we're going to have to do some serious negotiating."

I said it was fine with me, and as I drove that twisting road with the desperate caution of the slightly drunk, Charlie hung his head out the window and howled "Careless Love" to the black night and the silent trees.

We spent the next afternoon in a rehearsal hall, the largest of them, set deep in the woods. It was the only hall large enough to contain a piano. The negotiating we did concerned the Brahms sonata, and since we were on about the same level as sight readers, we got a decent fix on the first movement by the time the dinner bell rang. Charlie put his cello into its case.

"Want to take a bash at it after dinner?" he said.

"It'll be dark by then."

"We can play by kerosene lantern. There's a whole mess of them in the round barn."

Charlie and I skipped the evening performance to practice. He had checked with Theo to make sure the sound wouldn't carry to the chapel. We played in the faint light of the kerosene lamps, and many thousands of mosquitoes and moths gathered around to listen. At several of the more rhapsodic parts of the first movement, I was severely bitten on the forearm, elbow, and leg. When Charlie played, he closed his eyes and rocked the cello back and forth as if it were a child. There were times I lost my place just to look at him. We played for two hours and he worked up quite a sweat.

"I'd give anything to go swimming," I said.

"Let's do it," Charlie said. "We can have the pond all to ourselves."

"What about your cello?"

"Theo gave me a key, so I can lock it up."

"It's too early. There'll be people around."

"Come on, Elizabeth, you come up with some grand idea and then you squash it. Let's go."

I expected to see Laura and Giles, but there was no one there. The air was wet, and a thick mist had settled in. You couldn't even see the moon. We put our clothes on a flat stone and walked to the water's edge. Charlie put his foot in. "Oh my god," he said. "Cardiac gulch."

We joined hands and slid in. Icy water rolled over us.

"I knew I'd get you naked," Charlie said. I swam away from him and sat down on the grassy bank to dry, and watched him swimming toward me like a great friendly bear. When he got out, he shook the water out of his hair the way a dog will, and sat beside me.

"You're a tiny little thing," he said. "You don't act it, but you are."

I put my head on his large comfortable shoulder and began to cry.

"Look here," Charlie said. "I know you're a good and proper girl. It's no accident we found each other. Don't agonize. This isn't a tease. It's a swim."

He stroked my wet hair. "You tell Good Time Charlie Pepper what's on your mind," he said.

I told him about Patrick. I told him how frightened we were that Sam was between us and even though we thought we went deeper than that, we feared we were only refusing to admit it. I told him I thought that swimming naked with him was betraying Patrick.

"First of all, it's not your fault that he's your former brother in law," Charlie said. "Can't you just love him and not theorize? Can't you just go swimming without your clothes on and sit beside me because you want to? You aren't betraying Patrick. We've formed a friendship too, and this is part of it."

I said, "Charlie, you have a supple and loving heart."

"Only when stirred," he said. "Now, get your clothes on."

We walked toward the Victorian house his room was in, past the porch light and up the steps. In his room, he gave me a glass of whiskey. It seemed to me that I had never been so tired, tired of thinking, of reflecting, of turning life over and over in my mind. I curled up in an armchair and smoked a cigarette. Charlie sat in a rocker and smoked a cigar. The whiskey went directly to my head.

"I didn't come up here to mess around," I said.

"Good Christ, woman, neither did I."

"This isn't messing around, anyway," I said, pouring myself another shot.

"I want you to stay the night with me," Charlie said. "What do you want?"

"That's what I want."

"Maybe you'd like a couple of hours to think about it."

"You shut up. Don't make fun of me."

153

"You're so little I could flip you right over my shoulder and onto that bed with no more trouble than I'd swat a fly."

"It's only next to hulks like yourself that I'm small. Besides, I'm very strong." I stood up, trying to think of some demonstration of my strength, but I was interrupted by a knock on the door, and sat down unsteadily.

It was Corey Levenworth, Theo Zeller's overanxious assistant. He was a lean, athletic man with colorless spiky hair and pink plastic glasses. He wore chino pants with a knife-edge crease to them. During the year he was the director of a foundation that gave money to symphonies. He spent the summer with his wife and children on Martha's Vineyard and took off for a month to donate his time to the Conservatory. He had played the violin as a boy but he had given it up because he wasn't a genius, and he loved musicians, although at first glance it was hard to tell why he did. He looked like someone who had been born under the normal curve and what he liked to do best was administer. Theo was the genius of the Conservatory. He got people who had carried feuds for years to form string quartets and behave at dinner. But Corey was the Conservatory's dynamo, filled with health and energy, surrounded by a number of people who looked as if they had not been in the fresh air for many centuries and whom he felt he helped to function. His naïveté was breathtaking.

He found himself in Charlie's ill-lit room, confronted by a shirtless man and a clearly tipsy girl curled familiarly into a chair, but he was unstoppable, nonetheless.

"I saw the light on, and I thought I'd stop by since I've been looking for you two all day." He paused and squinted. "What luck to find you in the same place. Theo says you've been practicing some Brahms together, and I thought maybe you'd give a performance of it."

"Sure," said Charlie.

"No," I said.

"Come on, Elizabeth," Corey said. "Theo said he heard you walking past the hall and the sonata sounded good. You owe it to your fellows."

"Great idea," said Charlie.

"It's what we're here for," said Corey. "To learn from each other. Even our prodigies have something to learn."

He sat on the edge of the bed, as prim as a little tin soldier. The word for him was immaculate: he looked as if he had been dusted over with chalk, and he never appeared to sweat.

"I say yes," said Charlie. "What say, Elizabeth?"

I said okay, and Charlie gave me a fatherly wink.

"As long as I have you, Charlie," Corey said, "I'd really like to talk to you about the cello workshop."

"Fine, fine," said Charlie, reaching for the whiskey. "Drink?"

"Just a tiny one," said Corey.

I uncoiled my legs and stood up. Sitting there was too garish a gesture for me, even in front of a witless ninny.

"I'll walk you to the door," said Charlie. At the top of the stairs, he kissed me on my forehead.

"That's what we're here for," he said. "To learn from each other." He smiled at me across the banister.

"You'll pay for this," I said.

XVIII The next day, during a violent thunderstorm, Charlie and I had a fight in the library. He appeared at the door wearing a bright yellow slicker and carrying Anna Zeller's umbrella so he could walk in the rain and keep his cigar lit at the same time.

I said, "Why didn't you throw that motor moron out of your room last night?"

"Why the hell didn't you stay around?" Charlie said.

"If you're so hot on this ongoing friendship, why don't you implement it?"

"It's not my fault I got entangled in a bureaucratic net."

"Yes it is. You could have thrown him out. What the hell do you want from me, anyway?"

"I want your body in my arms. I'm in love with you."

"Well, if you're so in love with me, and so anxious to get my body in your arms, why did you let Corey get in the way of it?"

"I couldn't help it. What do you want from me?"

I looked out the window and watched a solid wall of rain bending the prehistoric ferns. There was a deep toll of thunder. I had never asked Sam what he wanted from me, or Patrick, nor had I wanted to be asked. These were not questions I thought proper in emotional life. I held to the rarefied notion that these things were known by intuition or not at all. I believed that love functioned on silent insight. What a foolhearted simp I was. The moment of my epiphany coincided with a flash of lightning—a truly banal example of the objective correlative—and I saw that I had lived a life of artful fear, that out of small-time terror I had fabricated my moral universe, in which you did not presume to ask the one you love what was expected of you or what you expected of him. I saw that I, cheering admirer, had given Sam license to be the reckless fool he was. I saw that out of my grand claim that you do not mess with the one you love, I had let the one I loved mess himself and me ultimately.

I thought of Patrick in my Cambridge kitchen wearing his mourning suit, saying, "It spared you the misery of eventual divorce." And I realized that half the reason I had let Sam be was to spare myself the witness of what he might have been unable to come up with. I couldn't have stopped him from doing anything, so I had taken myself out of the running and never asked at all, because it never occurred to me that Sam might make a gesture for me that was contrary to his nature. How very, very scared I was. I thought of Patrick, with whom I had managed to keep a lot of things tacit: I had thrown in my lot with him, and, so sure that love made everything understood, had never told him how much I loved him. I wanted us to live on some elevated, frictionless plane. I had never understood before that the love of another gives you ground to stand on: that it was not dishonorable to state the terms of love.

I said, "I want your friendship."

He said, "You've got it." And we clasped hands, like tycoons over a deal. At this point, we might have rushed out into the rain and up to Charlie's room, but instead we sat quietly in the library. Charlie sat in a wing chair by the window, watching the rain and smoking his cigar. It was so still that the smoke barely floated but hung above his head in a cloud the shape of a Portuguese man-of-war, and then dispersed.

My deep belief in the friendship between men and women grew out of an inactive kind of awe: theory was my safe haven, and appreciation is the safest thing on earth. You get to love and think about loving, and you might as well be conducting your life inside a hermetic bottle. For all my belief in emotional heroics, I liked a safe, static bet. Risk and intuition

157

are at the bottom of love, but slugging it out in the adult world is something else again, and I was neither skilled nor courageous at it.

I didn't plot for Sam—we went off like a pair of firecrackers. Patrick and I flared up like a fire—I didn't plot for him either. I didn't believe in plotting. It was wrong, I thought, to put strategy in the way of friendship. But the world was full of lovers laying their cards on the table, making demands, waiting to trap the ones they loved for good and proper reason and for a just and noble end. But I had never asked a thing, safe and snug under my blanket of moral justifying. All that flare and fire circumvented the cards upon the table. My moral nobility, my reluctance to take the chances the rest of the world took, I bottled and labeled and placed lovingly on the shelf with a tag reading *moral refinement.* But it was all dodge. Going off with Sam was a risk. That done, how dare I ask for more? The chances the rest of the world took were small time, like asking a husband to abandon his recklessness. The rest of the world said to its lover: "But what about me?" But I had never said it.

Patrick was my lucky star. He was the luckiest thing that had ever happened to me. I could ask Patrick anything if I wanted, but I hadn't wanted, so deep in thrall to things assumed. Assumption only *looks* safe; there isn't any safe and painless way to love. You have to stand and deliver, as the highway robbers say.

The room filled with cigar smoke and the rain began to lessen. A fine, damp breeze flooded in when Charlie opened the window. If we had been seen by a casual observer, he would have seen a man in a wing chair dreaming over his cigar and a girl in a Shaker replica rocker, reading. You could have used us for a painting called "Comfort and Yankee Weather."

The man in the chair was a married pediatrician and the girl was fresh from the arms of her brother-in-law, with whom she was in love. But personal history is nothing to a casual observer passing an occupied room by chance. We were not a couple enjoying the wetter part of the day. We were pending lovers, negotiating. I realized as I sat there that I was standing my ground. I wanted to know how serious Charlie was in order to decide how serious I would be. I wanted it stated, clear and simple. I thought how little I had asked from Sam, how, cowed in his presence and sure of my own correctness, I had made a judgment on him that made it unnecessary for him to act or me to expect it from him.

The bell rang for lunch. I had spent two weeks walking into the dining hall and waiting around to see where Charlie would place himself. I tried to make it all seem chance, since I assumed he would not want it publicly displayed that we were forming a friendship. But I was wrong. It hurt him. He said, "You make me feel it's an accident when you sit next to me at meals. I want you to sit next to me, for Chrissake."

How I did love cool and stealth. Weren't Sam and I cool and stealthy? Was it an accident that Patrick and I had not gone public? I thought of love as a concealed weapon against the world. So I stood on my side with my precise notions, and Sam stood on his side, thinking of love as a form of hub-cap stealing—something you got away with. And Patrick stood at the center of the universe, a patient man, full of propriety, which is only the marriage of stealth and caution. But Charlie Pepper was right out front. He was like a glass clock that showed you how it worked. He wanted me beside him, and if I wanted to sit with him at meals, why didn't I just sit? But I was of the watch-and-wait school of lovers. They watch, you wait, and when they give you a sign, you rush in.

We sat at an empty table and watched the hall fill up. Laura Zeller appeared and slumped into a chair.

"Giles is in one of his horrible moods," she said. "So if he comes to lunch, watch it." She stared abstractly into her water glass. Then she looked up. "He had a fight with Boris Dorfman and Corey about Prokofiev," she said, watching her hero stomp across the room. Even his hair looked furious. He was wearing a tee-shirt that had emblazoned across its front in red letters: *Aztec Airlines*.

He jerked back his chair and sat down. "Those guys are such antiquated fucking swine. Dorfman especially. Him and his

159

creepy tone poems and program music." He pushed his plate aside. "Those people are insane pigs. They don't like music. They like cartoons. I hate for music to be *about* anything."

"Giles got into trouble with the Toronto Symphony for refusing to play in the Carnival of the Animals when he was eight," Laura said.

"Let's get out of here," said Giles. "Let's grab some sandwiches in the barn and go down to the rehearsal hall and listen to you guys practice."

My heart failed. "I can't," I said. "I'm not going to be made a fool of in front of some boy genius."

Giles put his bony arm around my shoulder. "It's only music," he said, his face alight with the effort of his kindness. "Besides," he said, "I don't play duets."

Giles and Laura sat in the corner holding hands and Charlie and I played the sonata straight through. We creaked and stumbled, but on that afternoon we stopped playing our separate parts. It was a real duet. Between the first and second movements, Charlie took his pocket handkerchief and wrapped it around his neck, and after the second movement, he unwound it and tied it around my neck. It smelled of him, grassy and warm. He kissed me on the top of my head and I kissed him on the shoulder.

If love overcomes technique, the third movement was brilliant, mistakes and all. As I played, I could hear it: the spirit was right. When we were through, Charlie sighed and lay his bow across his knees. I slumped over the piano. The rain had made that hall like the inside of a steam room.

"That's pretty good," said Giles. Laura smiled faintly. "You guys are really lovely," she said.

In the afternoon, Charlie went to his cello workshop and I went back to the library. A large ginger cat was curled up in a chair, directly in a patch of sunlight. After the rain, the day had taken on a hazy red glow and the sun broke through the clouds in streamers. I sat and wrote Patrick a long letter addressed to his hotel in San Francisco. I told him about Laura and Giles and that I was going to play the Brahms E Minor cello sonata with a pediatrician from Knoxville. I told him how much I missed him and I told him that after a long spell I was taking music seriously again. But mostly I wrote a love letter. When I was by myself, I realized that I missed Patrick the way you would miss your arm if it were sheared off, or your eyesight, or your best friend.

I took my letter to the mailroom, and then strolled back to my cottage, where I found Libby Hayes bent over an air letter. She seemed to be in distress, but when she heard me coming up the path she raised her head, and I saw that she was laughing.

"My husband is the silliest man on earth," she said. "He's had the carpets taken up and he says it took six men and the au pair girl from next door to do it. What an amusing person he is. He says his arm is in plaster." Libby Hayes was a large woman with a chunky face. Her hair was pulled back into a chignon and she had beautiful white teeth, the shape of horse's teeth.

"Husbands aren't like other people," she said. "At least, not mine. A very strange breed, but then, of course, you've been spared this."

"I was married," I said.

She seemed surprised by this information.

"Oh, you young American girls," she said. "I keep forgetting. Everyone divorces these days."

"I was widowed."

"Oh. Quite," said Libby Hayes. "You also had this Vietnam business."

"Boating accident," I said, and went skipping up the stairs, as light as Libby's air letter.

When I got to my room, I saw that I was still wearing what was clearly Charlie's handkerchief around my neck. Charlie was a big-time brow mopper and those blue-and-yellow cloths were his alone. Libby Hayes had an eye out for what she called "the gossip of the place." It was her topic of conversation and she spoke of burgeoning relationships as if she were dealing with small animals dressed in children's clothes. "Isn't it sweet to see that nice little Tate girl going off with that clarinetist from Peabody," she remarked one afternoon, watching the

Conservatory's most pained and tortured pair walking down the road. To Libby Hayes, the world was full of garden gnomes. How nice to flash Charlie's kerchief in front of her. I saw her scan my wanton face and peg me as a fast little widow. What terrific copy for a letter to her husband.

What could I do? Sam was history. I honored and mourned him on my own time. It was a fact of the heart.

Charlie met me on the path, walking toward dinner, looking somewhere between sheepishness and grief.

I said, "What bureaucratic entanglement snared you for tonight?"

"I can't get away with anything around you," he said. "Theo asked me if I could put up some guy from the Boston *Globe* since all the guest rooms are full and my room is big enough for a cot."

"What a saint you are."

"Now, don't get petulant," he said. "I said we'd have our time together, and we will."

"You can go to hell," I said. "I'm going to the drive-in with Laura and Giles. You can shack up with the Boston *Globe* and I hope you two will be very happy together. I'm not going to grapple with a moral decision on your behalf if all you do is waffle out."

"What moral decision?"

"You said you wanted me. We're both people with deep commitments. I don't make decisions like this easily. I had to go through some hard times trying to figure out what was right. Now I've made up *my* mind, and now *you're* chicken."

"Our time will come," Charlie said. "I'll work it out."

"Not without me you won't," I said. "So long, sucker."

Giles and Laura and I sat through a five-year-old Western while necking couples steamed up the windows around us. Then we drove to Wrights' in Shortford and ordered burgers, with everything on, and they discussed the nature of their relationship.

Theo taught theory and composition at the Eastman Conservatory and Anna taught English at the University of Rochester. Giles' parents were both doctors in Toronto, so Laura and Giles weren't that far apart, but they got to see each other only on special occasions.

"I have three hundred letters from Giles," she said. "We sort of write a diary and send it to each other. Then we have to sneak, but it's a drag because we're both under age."

"Up here would be perfect if it weren't for all these creeps and morons," Giles said. "But at least they're all so self-absorbed that Laura and I can just disappear and nobody cares. If we make it to twenty, we're going to elope."

"I'll lend you my car," I said.

We drove back, but no one leaned out the window and sang "Careless Love." At the parking lot they kissed me good night and I watched them walk hand in hand down to the pond. When I got to my room, there was a note on my pillow:

> I'm at Zeller's drinking and mourning you.
> Come save me. I'm being held captive by the
> Boston *Globe*.

My first impulse was to go. My second was to take a shower and go to bed. There was plenty of time. That charming note annoyed me, but I was entitled, I felt, to a little righteous anger.

I slept the sleep of the just and innocent, but the next morning I was dragged away from my coffee by Charlie, who gathered me down to the rehearsal hall.

"You didn't come and get me," he said. "You're a heartless, ruthless woman. Why didn't you come and get me?"

"Why should I be tormented by the sight of what I can't have?"

He smiled his enormous smile. "I'm mightily glad you said that," he said.

We spent the day practicing, since we had just a week before the performance to get it perfect. After three hours of hard work, I looked around me and for an instant it was like coming out of a dream. Everything looked strange and new. The pines outside were not trees known to me. The room in which we sat was an alien structure and no place I had ever been before. Even Charlie was a stranger, sitting against the windowsill. The score in front of me was only a page of black, indecipherable marks, and when I came out of my dreamlike state I realized how little time we had left, how little time we had.

It had gotten uncommonly hot, so hot you could almost see the air. My shirt was sticking to me. Charlie mopped his forehead. When we looked across at each other, we were both exhausted, wiped out by heat and work. I looked at Charlie as if to memorize him forever, to imprint him in my vision so I would not lose him. I stared at the rafters and the beams of the rehearsal hall, at the hot, murky light the windows seemed to hold back. I wanted to fix it all forever, as I had not fixed Sam. I thought how careless I had been, thinking I had all the time in the world.

There Charlie sat. He was dreamy too. Beside the heat, beside our private histories and the mutual history between us, we were bound by the score of the Brahms sonata. I felt a great heave of tenderness for him, for his bulk and kindness, for the disk around his neck that announced his fatal vulnerability, for the family photos he kept in his wallet, for the kerchiefs he kept in his back pocket. I imagined him at the hospital surrounded by ailing children, and I imagined that if I were a sick child, I would want to hide myself inside his coat, secure against his ample frame.

I stopped watching him, stopped watching anything. His hand on my shoulder surprised me. Then I leaned my cheek against it.

I said, "Oh, Jesus. It's so sad," and stood up to put my arms around him, safe against his vulnerable bulk.

XIX The next morning all the mailboxes contained a grainy brown envelope. Inside, on brown paper, was an invitation to the Walter Marshalls' annual summer Conservatory party.

The Marshalls lived in Atlanta, but Reggie Marshall had grown up in Hamilton, and her father had been a trustee of the Conservatory. Their summer house was two miles up the road in Wycombe and every year students, teachers, visiting dignitaries, journalists, and performers gathered at the Marshalls' to raise a little hell.

The parties were famous—loud, boozy, and amalgamating. Everyone danced at the Marshalls'. Unlikely couples formed. There were kegs of very cold beer and buckets of fried chicken and the stereo blared out alternately rock and roll for the youthful and Dixieland or smooch music for the elderly. People who had been at the Conservatory over the years remembered their summers by the Marshalls' parties: the year the horn player from the Chicago Symphony lost both his shoes and found them hours later being worn by the cellist from the Gramercy String Quartet, or the year Boris Dorfman, that staid regular, had rumbaed a serious Formosan violinist out of the Marshalls' and into the night. Or the year there was a fistfight between two drunken conductors over an interpretation of Richard Strauss. Couples met at the Marshalls' parties and two years later married, or fought and six months later divorced.

The Marshalls were tall, leggy, and tanned, as if they spent their lives around horses and water; their manner was off-handedly cheerful and breezy. They dressed in silk and whipcord, like oversized jockeys. They were the sort of people who would know how to string up your hammock, or what to do if you broke your ankle in the woods or your horse died. Neither of them exuded the slightest glimmer of sexuality, and while neither of them was strikingly good-looking they had three beautiful teenaged daughters whose photos festooned the walls of their summer bedroom. These daughters were in Grenoble for the summer, perfecting their French. The Marshalls missed beauty by a fatal inch, and you could see how they would have gorgeous offspring.

Their house in Wycombe was a huge clapboard wedding cake set in a field. A columned porch wrapped around the house, and a set of outside stairs lead to a turret. The night of the party they hung yellow banners from their weather-vane.

I drove over with Theo, Anna, Laura, and Giles. Charlie had gone to get the beer. There were about a hundred and ten people there when we arrived, spilling out onto the lawn, shouting from the turret, gathered in clusters on the porch. The Marshalls invited not only the entire Conservatory but also their summer chums, and you could tell the summer chums by the bronze leather of their skins, and their clothes, which cost collectively what some of the staff made in a year. It was a sweltering night. The sky was more red than black. Charlie arrived and was pressed into service, unloading kegs of beer into washtubs of ice.

The party went in waves: the first to come and the first to leave were the Conservatory trustees, elderly formally dressed Yankees with white hair and summer dinner jackets or dresses with lace bosoms. With them left most of the older musicians. When they left, things loosened up and the younger and brasher of the staff began to dance, along with the teenage offspring of the Marshalls' summer friends. The Marshalls believed that you had to build a party up to any wildness, so they began with their beloved smooch music. Laura and Giles sat in the corner and watched Boris Dorfman dancing with Libby Hayes to Frank Sinatra.

"It's like watching a rabbit dancing with a cow," Giles said.

Charlie was exhibiting party behavior. Because he was big he was expansive, and you could tell that he had spent a lifetime discharging the responsibilities of his size—opening stuck windows, carrying the heaviest bundle, and making sure the homely and fainthearted had dancing partners. He danced with a solemn middle-aged Schubert scholar from Paris, who hardly spoke to anyone at all. He danced with Laura Zeller, smiling down on her, and with Anna. Then he danced with Reggie Marshall and they looked as if they had been born to dance together. They were a perfect fit. They seemed to have foxtrotted out of another era, some jovial, larky, well-intentioned time.

When the smooch music and Dixieland contingent gave up, the rock and rollers took over and I took my turn on the floor. During one slow, sultry number, Giles took me for a spin around the room and I was charmed by what was clearly dancing school training. By midnight the party was down to sixty and the room was lit by candles. The only lights on were in the kitchen, where the serious had gathered to talk and drink. Everyone was fairly drunk. From time to time, Laura and I collected bags of paper cups, beer cans, and chicken bones. The kegs had given out, and the Marshalls had broken open fifteen cases of beer.

As it got later, it got hotter. It seemed about to rain. The lit ends of cigarettes dotted the porch, and one could see the red point of a reefer being passed hand to hand. The living room was full of dreamy couples, swaying back and forth on the dance floor, and people sitting in twos on the floor with their arms entwined. Finally Charlie claimed me and we cleared a little space to dance. I was past care, so I wrapped myself around him like a vine. Everyone was far too drunk to notice, and if they noticed, so what? This would be the party at which that young widow got drunk and made a fool of herself with Charlie Pepper.

We danced until the heat drove us outside, where we sat on the porch steps to smoke. Then we walked into the field until, when we looked back, only the candlelit windows were visible in the distance. The grass was wet and long and we walked through it like explorers. The mosquitoes were severe. "These mothers are the size of Cadillacs," said Charlie, slapping. The sky was hazy except for a glimmering, veiled spot where the moon burned dimly through. The earth was steaming and the air was as palpable as fruit.

Charlie put his heavy arm around me. I moved closer and he took my hand.

"That's a little paw to fit around me," he said.

"It'll fit."

"You're in my bloodstream," he said. "This is serious."

We stood in that field surrounded by crickets, sniped by savage mosquitoes. I wanted to stand there forever in the midst of that heat, listening to distant thunder with Charlie Pepper pressed to me. Standing on my toes, I could put my arm around his neck.

"Say you love me," said Charlie.

I said I did.

We walked back slowly. A boy was sleeping on the porch. The same couples were sitting, stoned, in wicker chairs. The dancing in the living room was more like clinging: those drunken twosomes were beginning to wilt. Half an hour later I left alone and walked the two miles back. The air was so wet it swirled in front of me. There was not a car on the road, not a star in the sky. I had a patch of the night to myself, and I breathed it in—earth and pine. Then I saw the lights ahead of me and walked slowly toward Charlie Pepper's room. All around me were dreaming musicians, sleeping with their lawful spouses, I thought, or sharing the night with no one. Chaste girls sat with their desk lamps on, studying the *Kindertotenlieder*. Back in my cottage Libby Hayes was doubtless writing a letter to her amusing husband. I was sure there was a rightful place for everyone, and if there was sinning going on at the Hamilton Conservatory I didn't think of it. I wanted to be the only sinner afoot in that sleepy landscape, and if Giles and Laura lay wrapped together under a blanket by the pond, it was sweetness that connected them, not stealth.

A lamp glowed on the porch of Charlie's house, circled by gnats. There was a light on in his room—I could see it from the road. As I walked under the porch light, the light made me feel publicly baptized. There was not a soul around. I crept up the stairs, shoes in hand, as quiet as an Indian, trying to find the spot on each stair that didn't creak. All the rooms had large oak doors, and as I turned the knob to Charlie's, the lock clicked and the door whined. It seemed an enormous noise. Dampness had made the door stick, so I finally had to shove it open with my shoulder.

His leather suitcase was lying on its side and his cello case was propped against the wall. The bed was made, but he had napped on it, and the spread was dented and wrinkled where his shape had been. The desk lamp was on, casting a dingy, blue light. A huge moth beat its wings against the screen. How melancholy it all looked. On the desk were two wrinkled shirts and his bow. Next to his pillow was the Brahms score: he must have been studying it before he napped. On the dresser were his brush and comb, a bottle of vitamin pills, a bottle of whiskey, and a roll from dinner, as hard as a stone.

I sat down on the side of the bed and put my face to his pillow, hoping his scent would still be there, grassy, smoky, and pungent. For all his artifacts, that room was as bare as a cell—it wasn't his room, even for the box of cigars on the night table or his stack of checked handkerchiefs. It had oak floors and oak beams and the bed had a maple headboard. On the floor was a hooked rug. But still, it had the air of a cheap hotel, the sort of place renegade lovers go to crash.

I heard a car go over gravel and stop. I heard Charlie saying goodnight. The car door closed. He took the creaking stairs slowly, and as I waited for him, I felt a pang of longing. He walked in and found me standing by his bed, but he didn't greet me, or even speak. He looked tired, hot, and terribly sad. He sat down and held out his arms.

"You better come over here quick," he said. "I'm feeling very melancholy." I stood in the circle his arms made. "Let me see you. Let me see how melancholy you are." I put my arms around him. If there was something on my face for him to read, I didn't know what it was.

I said, "While I was waiting for you, I missed you."

He said, in the voice of an exhausted host whose guests have stayed too long, "Let's go to bed."

Toward morning it began to storm and I woke up. The faint light reflected off the stained floor and tinted everything orange. Charlie's arm encircled me. I was pinned to his side. All you could hear was the sound of rain being pushed through the trees and the steady drum of water on the roof. The thunder was like a low cough in the next room. All I felt was a sense of correctness and, snuggling closer to its source and focal point, I went back to sleep.

It was still raining when we got up. The breakfast bell rang, but neither of us stirred. Charlie had a cheap electric kettle and some instant coffee and we drank, propped by pillows. Down the hall, Billy Henshaw began to play the clarinet. We heard a sharp knock at his door and the playing stopped.

Charlie said, "Are you going to tell Patrick about this?"

"Eventually. Are you going to tell Mary Beth?"

"No."

"A lot of people would think this makes us a pair of true betrayers," I said.

"This is between you and me," said Charlie.

I said, "If I hadn't met you, Charlie, I don't know that I would have known very much about me and Patrick. If I hadn't met up with you, there are things about him I never would have known, or things about myself. Being with you doesn't shake my ties to him. It affirms them. I'm right to love him, and I'm right to love you. You've been a great friend to me. I'm glad this happened. I was balky about Patrick, with Sam in that straight line."

"We're a very unsentimental pair," said Charlie.

"This is better," I said.

XX We were set to play the Brahms sonata the last week of the Conservatory. At every turn, Corey Levenworth nipped at our heels, clucking like an old hen. He nudged us toward the rehearsal hall, and if he saw us without a score in hand, he looked amazed and disappointed. We were his wayward sheep and he was the chinoed, pink-spectacled sheepdog leading us to our rightful place. He was the sort of man who looked you straight in the eyes and then consulted his watch: Corey's life was made up of minutes. His present worry was that the sonata wasn't long enough for an entire program, but that was settled by Laura and Giles.

They appeared at the rehearsal hall one afternoon and leaned against the window making faces against the glass until Charlie looked up and told them to come in.

"We have a confession to make," Giles said. He was wearing his Aztec Airlines tee-shirt. Laura wore a blouse with butterflies embroidered on it.

"You have a confession," Laura corrected.

"Well, I lied," he said. "I was being snotty when I said I didn't play duets, because I do, but only with Laura."

Charlie and I looked puzzled. "She plays the violin, but she's very shy about it. She's good, too. So we figured that maybe I would stop being snotty and she would stop being shy and we could play a little Schubert sonatina on the same program. We heard Corey talking to Theo, see. If you wouldn't mind, of course."

"Perfect," said Charlie.

"Perfect," I said.

"It's the one in A," said Laura. "I always think of Giles when I hear it because Schubert was only nineteen when he wrote it. We've been playing it for three years. We always play it when we get together."

So it was set. The news delivered, Corey stopped clucking and Charlie and I were left to our own devices. These devices included five hours a day practice. We played after dinner, after the performance, and then we executed a neat social ritual at the Zellers'. At an arbitrary point in the evening, I left, having kissed the cheeks and shaken the hands of the assembled worthies and walked, as brazen as a pot, to Charlie's room, where I amused myself by reading *David Copperfield* until he saw fit to leave. Thus the affair between the fast little widow and the nice big cellist was not thrown into the face of the populace at large. No one noticed.

No one noticed and no one cared, and if they had noticed, they probably would have thought it a nice thing to happen to two nice people, but my sense of propriety and my taste for the clandestine were like a genie let out of its bottle. Affairs had been conducted at the Conservatory and would continue to be. The gossip and rumor mill was subtle but effective. For a few days I was positively hagridden by the notion of appearing to be in sleazy fly-by-night circumstances, and then I stopped caring; but I still kept up my ritual.

The morning of the performance I woke up shaky. It was a bright, gray day. When I heard the breakfast bell ring, I buried my head against Charlie's chest and began to cry.

"Don't you worry about tonight," he said. "We'll do just fine. We've got it perfect."

"It's not the music."

There were tears in his eyes too. "No, it's not the music," he said.

"But we beat the clock, didn't we, Charlie?"

"Yes," he said sadly. "We outfoxed time itself."

We practiced that morning and in the afternoon we took a walk through the field, through the birch stand, and into the woods. We sat on two flat rocks and dipped our naked feet into the icy stream. Whirlpools of gnats circled the water. We sat for a long time without speaking. Walking back, in the birch stand Charlie picked me up and threw me over his shoulders. He held me upside down by my ankles and shook me. Dimes and quarters fell out of my pockets and onto the forest floor.

"It's not often you get to turn the one you love upside down," Charlie said.

By sundown we had severe jitters. Charlie paced up and down in his room like a caged cat. I asked him if he wanted to be left alone.

"Do you?" he said.

I said, "We have two hours. It's just dinnertime. I'm going to skip dinner and get dressed, but I'd like to spend the last hour before countdown with you."

"Perfect," he said.

We spent the last hour in his room. He was shirtless and still stalking.

I said, "If you don't sit down, I'm going to tackle you."

"You and how many others your size," he said, but he sat in a rocking chair and threw his nervous energy into that. "I haven't performed alone in a mighty long time. Let's take a bath."

"We can't take a bath," I said. "We're dressed. Have a little mercy, will you? I haven't played seriously for over a year. I haven't played in public for two years. If you're edgy, we can have a fight about what shirt you're going to wear."

"I'm going to wear a pink shirt to match your dress. I think that's fitting and proper."

There were two bells before the performance. One was rung fifteen minutes before and one five minutes before. When the first bell rang, Charlie put on his shirt.

"Okay, Mrs. Elizabeth. This is it," he said.

"Okay. Let's go."

"Not before I kiss you." He kissed me and buttoned his shirt. "We're in this together," he said, and we walked to the chapel clutching our scores. Giles and Laura were on first, so Charlie and I sat in the front row, sharing an armrest. The second bell rang and the little chapel filled up.

Corey introduced Laura and Giles. For the occasion he had put on a Madras sports jacket so crisp and sharp you could have sliced yourself on its sleeve. The lights dimmed. Laura wore a silk blouse with hearts embroidered on it, and Giles wore a white shirt. They nodded to each other and began.

You could tell why the Schubert sonatina reminded Laura of Giles. It sounded like a mournful love letter, interrupted by fits of overwrought hopefulness. Laura looked wholesome and serious. She had pinned her braid into a coil at the back of her neck. Her eyes were closed. Giles swayed away from the piano as he played. The music took them over and seemed to play through them. I imagined them at thirteen, using that music as a salute when they met. Hearing that music played by them was like having honey poured all over you. The audience was rapt.

Giles and Laura got a lot of mileage out of the sweeter parts, but in the *allegro vivace*, you could see they were both prodigies. Theo and Anna wore on their faces expressions of such fierce pride it was hard to look at them. Even Boris Dorfman, upon whom Giles so loved to vent his hostility, was captivated. Corey looked as if tenderness were breathing heavily down the neck of his crisp shirt. You felt that instead of applauding, the entire audience would rush to the front of the chapel and smother them with kisses. The oldest member of the conservatory, Dr. Henrich von Arnheim, who had the *Deutsche Allgemeine Zeitung* airmailed to New Hampshire, who was eighty years old and had fled the Nazis, who was known to his students at Berkeley to be a passionate taskmaster, looked as if he had fallen in love for the first time.

When they finished, Giles bounced up from the piano and grabbed Laura's hand. The audience cheered. Theo put his arm around Anna and drew her close.

"This is some act to follow," Charlie said.

Immaculate Corey introduced us. Charlie and I clasped

hands. I must have walked to the piano, because I found myself sitting at it, wondering what to do with all those keys. Twenty years of musical training fell away from me. Charlie picked up his bow and we began.

So there we were, in that gray-and-white chapel, playing our hearts out. Charlie was right: we did have it perfect. We could have played it in our sleep. That music was our get-off point, but it was friendship that held us. It occurred to me that Sam soldered Patrick and me together in the same way. It was the bond that mattered, not what tied it up. Sam was a fact of life, like music.

We seemed to have just started. The first and second movements went by. Halfway through the third movement I realized we were almost through. How nice it would have been to sit snug in the audience so I could see how we were doing, but then it was over. Charlie placed his bow on his knees and mopped his brow. We both stood up and the look that we exchanged was one of triumph and weariness. Then there was a great cheer. Giles leaped to his feet. The audience was such a blur I could only make out Laura and Giles. I stood next to Charlie by the piano. They were standing and cheering and for an instant it seemed that they were cheering us not for the music but for ourselves.

Outside, Laura and Giles and Charlie and I were surrounded. Heinrich von Arnheim kissed us all. "It is a privilege to be witness to that devotion," he said.

Laura whispered, "Giles and I are going to the pond."

Charlie said, "We'd better put in an hour at your parents' so we can be properly congratulated."

So we walked to the Zellers', the four of us, arm in arm.

XXI The last week, Corey Levenworth took photographs. He ran around with his Nikon, snapping madly. He got a shot of Giles and Laura under a tree, of Libby Hayes having her lunch, of Boris Dorfman wearing a straw hat, of Heinrich von Arnheim reading his *Deutsche Allgemeine*, of Laura and Giles performing the Schubert, of me and Charlie performing the Brahms. He surprised me in the library one sunny afternoon and clicked off four shots.

"What perfect light!" he shouted, exiting.

I said to Charlie, "Perhaps you'd like to invite him up to your room so he can get a shot of this year's most illicit couple."

I watched Corey scamper around, the caretaker's dog at his feet and his camera bouncing against his chest. I hated the neatness with which he thought he could catalogue his life. He would pass his less crowded winter evenings pasting his summers into his scrapbook. I wondered if there was anything in his life that couldn't be codified or stapled down, something he didn't have a photo of, or document referring to, an event he had to summon up in painful memory. He squinted into the sun, and on the very brightest days he wore a pot hat. I expected him to have a whistle suspended from a string around his neck, but there was only his camera, that intrusive lavaliere.

But then I relented. Poor Corey was only hedging his bets. He loved the Conservatory, truly. It wasn't entirely his fault he was a drip and innocent. I hated his innocence only because I felt so lost from my own, but those photos probably sustained

176

him, and I knew that some October morning, I would find in my mailbox a manila envelope, and inside would be a set of Corey's photos, for me to put in my scrapbook.

Charlie and I went shopping in Milford Haven, for our loved ones.

He said, "This is a photo entitled 'The Errant Lovers Shop for Their Spouses.'"

We were standing in front of an old weathered barn outside of which were stacks and piles of junk, inside of which was the high-priced stuff: New England antiques. From the junk, I bought for Patrick a poker in the shape of a pitchfork, the handle of which was a crow with outstretched wings. Inside, Charlie bought a quilt for Mary Beth and I bought Patrick a schoolhouse clock. Then we drove to the general store, where Charlie bought spruce gum and maple sugar for his children. We had our lunch at Wrights', in Shortford. Charlie held my hand and smoked his cigar.

"Are you sorry?" he said.

"I'm not sorry about anything. I'm not sorry I'm going back. It's right to be going back. But I'll miss you."

"What will you do?"

"Well, first of all, Patrick and I are going to announce ourselves to our parents. Then I'm going to apply to Juilliard. I'm tired of research. If I can't be a performer, I'll write about music, or I'll find some sympathetic quintet to play with. And you?"

"My life is cut out pretty nicely. I've got Mary Beth and the kids, and the hospital and the symphony. A nice life. But I'll think about you."

"Charlie, can we write to each other once in a while?"

"It never occurred to me that we wouldn't," he said.

The last days sped by, as last days do. I felt that I had just arrived, and when I got to my unlived-in room I realized that I was ready to pack and say goodbye. I had an urge to press wildflowers into my book, to steal the score of the Brahms sonata, the pillow case from Charlie's bed. I was much soupier than Corey Levenworth would ever hope to be. You have to commit experience to your heart and let it change you, I knew, but for all that, the first thing I packed was Charlie's handkerchief. My open suitcase lay on my bed, but my room wasn't melancholy—nothing had ever happened in it.

I kept a few minutes to myself and sat in my assigned room. I realized how bitter I had been, bitter that life gave you love and good times and then whisked them away. How bitter I had been that Sam was memory, had been made into memory. Now I was faced with Charlie, who would be memory too, but my bitterness had fallen away from me. I had put myself in the way of certain pain, but I was right to. Sam had marked me with my first sense of loss and I would always keep it with me, but it didn't stand between me and the world, or between me and Patrick. Sam was my lark in the world, and I would never have known my own measure if it had not been for him. But Patrick tested my depth. He was the line I threw over the side to see how deep the water was, but Charlie tugged the line and then I knew how deep I ran.

The last meal at the Conservatory was formal. The dining hall was decked with branches of pine. There were white cloths on the table, candles, and vases of wildflowers. Corey Levenworth had ordered fifteen cases of champagne.

At dinner, Charlie and I sat with Theo and Anna, Laura and Giles. Laura's eyes glowed and she dropped her head on Giles' shoulder by the time dessert came around. After dinner, Theo made a speech and said this year had been the Conservatory's finest.

"He says that every year," Laura whispered.

"But this year it's true," Charlie said.

After dinner, it was ritual for the entire group to go to the round barn. Traditionally there was a fire in the fireplace if it was cold enough, and a great bowl of punch. For an hour you stood and socialized. Then Theo sat to the piano and the old regulars clustered around to sing "Come Ye Sons of Art."

We drank our punch and said our goodbyes. It was to be an early night.

Giles said, "I hate goodbyes. Laura and I are going to split, unless you want to come to the pond with us."

"They don't want to, silly," said Laura.

He shook Charlie's hand gravely, but Charlie threw an arm around him and gave him a bear hug. We stood in a loving circle, then walked them to the door of the barn and watched them go off hand in hand toward the pond. I went to call Patrick and Charlie went to call Mary Beth. Then we met at the Zellers' for a last drink and to write addresses into our notebooks. I stayed an hour and left, saying my courtly goodbyes. Out in the darkness, I looked toward Charlie's room. It took all my courage to cross the road, to pass myself under the scrutiny of that porch lamp. Everyone, I thought, was up and watching, but it wasn't paranoia, it was sadness. This was my last trot up those stairs.

When Charlie came back, I was sitting in his rocker. His suitcase and cello were packed. Only the bottle of whiskey and the vitamin pills were out.

"I'm set," he said. "Tickets. Money. Keys. I remember my name and home address. Mary Beth is meeting me at the plane. You still want to lug this old bear to Kennedy Airport?"

"That was settled a long time ago," I said. "Don't you remember?"

"I can't remember anything," he said. "Except you sitting here. Did you get Patrick?"

"He's going to Washington for the day, so we'll get back at about the same time."

Charlie sighed heavily, so heavily I laughed and hugged him.

"You heartless New York girls," he said. "Laughing at a stricken man."

"I've been sighing all day, but you can't hear it since I'm so small."

"You small, heartless New York girls. Come over here and put yourself in Good Time Charlie's lap, before he dies of sorrow."

I coiled my arms around him and we sat in the rocker without speaking.

"Do you want to leave before or after breakfast?" he said.

179

"Before. We can have breakfast on the road."

"That's fine," he said. "The last face I want to see around here is yours."

It was an early night only for us. All around were the sounds of bags being slammed shut, dragging luggage, giggles, and murmured conversations. From up the road came the sound of singing.

We lay in the quiet of our own last night, and fell asleep.

We were up with the light, and Charlie boiled water for coffee. We were both intensely cheery until it was time to leave that room and pull the car around so we could load our bags. I balked at the doorway, weepy and swept with shame. He stroked my hair.

"Don't be bashful," he said. "It isn't sentiment. Something happened to us." When I looked up, there were tears in his eyes too.

"Come on, now," he said. "Let's hit it."

We dragged his cello case and bag down to the porch and went to the parking lot to get the car. Everyone at my cottage was still asleep and we walked carefully up the steps to get my bag. We loaded the car and took off. Charlie drove with one hand on the wheel and one hand clamped to mine.

We decided to take not the Interstate but the scenic route instead, and we stopped at a little town to have our breakfast in the diner. In one booth a group of locals wearing jodhpurs were drinking beer with their scrambled eggs and hooting.

We ordered a massive breakfast. There was a sheen on everything, on that cheap Formica table, on the dented cream pitcher, on those horsey locals in their muddy boots. I thought I would keep it with me forever, the faint whiff of horse the place exuded, the faded design on the plates.

As I looked at Charlie, looming up on his side of the table, I felt something very close to gratitude, but it was only love and respect, mixed with something in me that he had freed and enlightened. If you can drink life in, I drank. I drank to love and death and friendship, to loss and complication, to deprivation and wisdom.

We polished off that breakfast like a pair of tigers and went through two pots of coffee. Charlie sat back in his chair, smoking a cigar. There was nothing specious in my happiness. It rang through me like a bell.

Charlie and I sat smoking with our legs entwined, and I knew what it would be like to leave him at the airport, that I would not watch him off, and that in the car, alone, I would not feel sadness, but an affirming calm, the result of any dignified decision of love and friendship. I could see him in my mind, walking to the checkout gate. I could see him on the stairs to the plane, ducking slightly as he made his way to his cramped seat. I saw him doze through takeoff and then wake up as the stewardess tapped his arm to see if he wanted coffee. I could see him watch the clouds part, and knew that he would see the plane casting on the green and yellow earth the wavering, moving shadow of itself.